Steamboat Willie Whistlestop Puzzle Mysteries, Vol. 1

HANNAH DOVE

PLOTWORKS PUBLISHING

Introduction

Welcome to the world of *Steamboat Willie Whistlestop Puzzle Mysteries*!

It's the 1920s, and you're the new first mate of a steamboat, the SS Wilkinshire. Willie is a talking mouse who you'll encounter on your first mystery!

Together, the two of you will solve crimes.

And there's a lot of them! The SS Wilkinshire is a magnet for unfortunate events: murder, blackmail, thievery. There's always a puzzle that needs to be solved.

If you think playing detective is going to be easy, think again! These puzzle mysteries are tricky. It takes a very sharp eye to recognize the clues, so read carefully!

In each puzzle mystery, you and Steamboat Willie will first discover the crime. Then you'll speak to each suspect. One by one, they'll explain their alibis in detail. After that, you'll have the option to read the hint, which is conveniently hidden at the back of the book.

Finally, when you think you know the identity of the culprit, turn to the solution!

Ready?

Let's go!

Enjoy your crime-solving trip down the river with everybody's favorite mouse, Steamboat Willie!

Case #1: The Captain's Gift

THERE'S a lump in your throat as you walk toward the large ship docked at the end of the harbor. You wonder if your decision to become first mate on a steamboat was a bit hasty. You're the type who enjoys quiet afternoons, curled up with a book or a puzzle. Spending your days scrubbing decks, catering to demanding passengers, and tossing coal into the boilers isn't your idea of a fun job. But after what happened to your father, you need the money.

At the back of the steamboat, you recognize a large man with a red beard and a fine white hat. Captain Ewan is the one who conducted your interview. He called you a landlubber, called you a fool for applying, and then asked when you could start. It was more than a bit peculiar, and you're not quite sure what to think of him.

"Welcome aboard the SS Wilkinshire," he announces, patting your shoulder with a bit too much force as you walk up the gangplank.

You stumble forward, almost dropping the small bag that holds your belongings. Your eyes go to the wooden planks that make up the steamboat's deck. You think you see something small and black scurry behind a barrel.

Before you can investigate, Captain Ewan puts his arm around your shoulders and forces you to walk forward. You notice that the tip of his nose is bright red and his round cheeks are flushed.

"Let me introduce you to the rest of the crew. After that, I have a gift for you." He winks at you, and you smell the whisky on his breath.

Good thing you won't be setting sail until tomorrow.

The Captain takes you below deck to the crew's quarters. "First stop is the men's room," he announces, knocking loudly before pushing a small wooden door open.

Beyond is a small cabin with a bunk bed with two narrow built in closets on either side. A small table has been squashed into the corner by the door. Two men perch on little stools before it. One is large with bright blue eyes, a black beard, and a scar across his cheek. The other resembles a mouse, with a long nose, loose brown hair, and dark, shifting eyes. A lollipop stick protrudes from the corner of his lips.

You've caught them in the middle of an argument.

"Could've at least let me help instead of making me sit in a corner and watch," the mousy one protests, lollipop stick twitching as he speaks.

Black beard snorts. "Absolutely not. I know what a sweet tooth you have. You'd have swiped some of it without a second thought, you pilfering little—"

"Ahem!" The Captain interrupts them with a loud whisky-scented cough. "Our new first mate is here. Perhaps we want to make a better introduction."

The two men stop fighting and finally notice you standing behind the Captain. You wave in greeting.

Black beard stumbles to his feet. He's so tall, he has to

stoop to avoid banging his head on the ceiling. You wonder how he manages to survive on such a small boat.

"Joe Steely," Black beard introduces himself. "I'm the resident chef on the SS Wilkinshire. Honor to have you aboard." He holds out his hand, and you shake it. There's powder on his hand.

When you look down at your fingers after, you see that they've been stained with something brown.

"And I'm Biggie O'Toole," the mousy one says. He doesn't stand up, but salutes you from his stool, leaning back as much as he can in the cramped space. "Been wondering when you'd arrive. You a fan of sweets?"

His eyes flick toward the bottom bunk. There's a large glass jar with an assortment of sweets.

Your eyebrows rise.

Biggie's lips quirk upward in a smile. He takes the lollipop out of his mouth. "Figured. But don't take any of mine. Even if you is the first mate."

The Captain scolds Biggie for his rudeness and hurries you out the room.

"Don't mind Biggie. He'll warm up to you. All the crew will." He turns away and mutters under his breath, "Eventually."

The two of you visit the girls' room next. It's only a few steps further down the passage.

Captain Ewan knocks again before opening the door.

The cabin within is identical to the one you just visited. Only there's a rather unpleasant smell. You try to breathe in through your mouth, wondering if it has to do with the woman lying on the bottom bunk. She's rather large with dark hair and a forehead covered in sweat.

"Awful isn't it," a young, straw-haired blonde says, holding her nose and making a face as she steps out from behind the door. "I've had to do her job all day and care for her. She's drank so much water the river might run dry."

To prove her point, the blonde points to a cup resting precariously on the edge of the bed frame. The glass has a brown, sweat-covered smudge.

"My goodness," the Captain says. "It's food poisoning again, isn't it? Estelle, you know you aren't supposed to eat dairy." There's a concerned look in his gaze as he studies his sick crew member.

"It's Joe's fault," Estelle moans. "He probably put milk in the eggs this morning." She sits up and notices you for the first time. Her groaning stops, and suddenly, she doesn't seem quite as violently ill. "Who's this?"

"Our new first mate," the Captain introduces you to the two women. "Estelle is our cleaner, and Gertie is our errands girl. She fills in wherever she's needed."

"I prefer to think of myself as a waitress," the blonde, Gertie, informs you. "It's the most glamorous of my tasks."

You shake her hand. It's slightly damp, and smells faintly of soap.

The Captain keeps the rest of the introduction brief, probably looking for an excuse to escape the rather foul-smelling room. He takes you a few steps further toward your cabin.

There's only one bed pressed against the wall. The rest of the space is filled with a built-in dresser and small desk. It's not much larger than the crews' cabins, but at least it's clean, and you won't have to share.

Captain Ewan points to a silver box on top of your pillow. "That's a little something for you to welcome you to the team. I rested it there less than an hour ago, so it shouldn't have melted. I do hope you like it." He nods at you. "I'll leave you to settle in."

You thank him, and his cheeks turn red as though he's not used to gratitude from his crew.

Once you're alone, you drop your small bag on the desk, lift up your present, and open the box.

It's empty.

"There was a bar of chocolate in it," a small voice informs you.

A shiver tickles the back of your neck. Your eyes dart around the room. There's no one else with you.

Could it be a ghost?

"Psst, down here."

You follow the sound of the voice to the foot of the bed. Something small and black scurries onto your sheets until it stops on your pillow.

Your eyes grow wide.

Sitting on your bed, grinning up at you is a mouse, dressed in a yellow rain jacket and holding a piece of cheese. He crosses his legs, leans back on your pillow just like a human, and continues to talk.

"Who are you?" you ask.

"Name's Steamboat Willie," the mouse replies. "I've been on this ship for the past year, so I know all about how things work. Crew is full of thieves, every whistlestop brings some disaster, and more than a few people have died aboard. I'll bet Captain Ewan left all that out when he offered you the job. But don't feel bad. Now you know the truth, you can run along and quit and leave me in my room in peace." He closes his eyes, wiggling his butt against your pillow.

When he opens them, he sees you still standing in the room.

"Huh? Why aren't you running? Are you slow?" he asks, giving you a puzzled look. "The last few first mates bolted the moment they heard me, but you don't seem terrified of a talking mouse. Maybe you're different. Tell you what, I'll let you share my room if you can pass my test. Think you're up for it?"

You shrug.

Your Answer

WHO STOLE THE CHOCOLATE?

1. Joe
2. Biggie
3. Estelle
4. Gertie

If you need a hint, turn to the back of this book.
If you know the culprit, turn the page for the solution.

The Solution

Answer: Gertie

SINCE GERTIE WAS DOING the cleaning for Estelle, she's the only one who had any reason to enter your room and discover the Captain's gift. Plus, there was a brown smudge on the glass that Gertie gave to Estelle. The stain was likely chocolate that was on Gertie's hands before she washed them.

Plus, we know from their argument that Joe and Biggie were together most of the day. As the chef, the brown powder on Joe's hands was most likely cocoa powder that he'd used in whatever dessert Biggie wanted to steal.

Estelle could've eaten the chocolate and gotten sick, but we know that she's been sick since that morning since Gertie did her job.

"I knew you could figure it out!" Willie says. "There's something about you that I like. So, I'll let you stay. You can be my assistant. I'm something of a detective. Stick with me, and we'll get our first case soon."

A smile plays on your lips as you unpack your suitcase.

You were expecting to be first mate on a steamboat, but now your path has taken an unexpected turn.

You've just met a talking mouse. And he's a detective.

Case #2: A Mysterious Drowning

YOU'VE BARELY BEEN WORKING on the SS Wilkinshire for a week when the first incident occurs. Business tycoon Clyde Mill falls from the steamboat and drowns in the river.

You stand beside Captain Ewan by the wheel. Willie is hiding in your sleeve. His nose pokes out, unnoticed, as you both watch the scene unfolding on the front deck. Biggie and Joe are attempting to fish the body from the river while a group of passengers watch with morbid curiosity a few feet behind.

Among them, you recognize one of Mr. Mill's traveling companions. His secretary Martha Green dabs her eyes with a tissue.

Willie crawls up your sleeve to sit on your shoulder, hidden by the tall white collar of your uniform.

"Funny that the secretary's here, but not the other three," he whispers. "Where do you suppose they are?"

You try to recall who Willie is referring to.

Mr. Mill rented the four largest rooms on the ship in celebration of his anniversary with his wife, Veronica. However, they were the only couple. The other three rooms were taken by individuals: his secretary Martha Green, his son Henry Mill, and business partner Dennis Wads.

"I think something suspicious is afoot," Willie whispers, rubbing his paws together. "Mr. Mill didn't just fall over the side of the boat. I think that he was pushed."

* * *

You and Willie start your investigation down on the deck.

The crowd has been ordered below deck where Joe is serving breakfast. It's only Biggie that remains outside with the corpse.

"What're you doing here?" he asks, narrowing his dark eyes. "Suppose you got curious too. Well, go on then, poke around if you must. Not much of interest. Obviously the poor bugger got drunk, fell over the railing, and drowned. Lucky we were in a shallow part and were able to recover the body at all."

You kneel down to examine the corpse.

Clyde Mill is puffy and bloated. He still has on his outfit from the previous night: a white shirt with a dark pair of pants, rolled around his ankles. His lips are parted.

"There's something in his mouth," Willie whispers.

You follow the mouse's instructions, open the mouth, and find a ball of fabric shoved within.

"Hey, what're you doing? We're not supposed to touch —" Biggie begins to object until he sees what it is you're pulling out. "Blimey, is that a tie?"

It is. In your hands is a long, red silk tie with the crest of a swan stitched in yellow.

Biggie's eyes are wide as he stares at it. "Don't think I've ever seen such a nice one in my life. Is it silk? Bet it's worth more than a penny. We could keep it and sell it, you know."

Your eyes narrow at Biggie.

He holds up his hands. "All right. All right. It was only a joke."

You're not entirely sure that it was. But Biggie's willingness to tamper with evidence isn't nearly as pressing as investigating Clyde Mill's death. There's less than an hour before you get to the dock, and the police will be waiting there. The Captain already radioed ahead and told them it was an accident. They might not do a thorough investigation, and then the culprit will be free.

You ask Biggie to walk you through what happened this morning that led to the discovery of the body.

"It was around five in the morning. I was lying in my bed, trying to sleep in, but that's almost impossible for me. I'm a light sleeper. Anyway, I heard that woman, what's her name, the young, pretty blonde secretary with the big... oh right, Martha. Anyway, she was shouting for Mister Mill, sounded real desperate. I can't bear to hear a lady in distress, so I put on my best shirt and came out to help, real gentleman-like, you know.

"The two of us searched the ship for him. He wasn't in his room. Only his wife, Veronica was in there, passed out drunk, or at least pretending to be. We had to force the door.

"He wasn't with his son or business partner either, but they got up to help us. Then, after a bit of searching, Mister Wads says, 'You don't suppose he fell overboard, do you?'

"And his son gets this scared look on his face and says, 'He won't have survived if that happened. He can't swim.'

"'I know,' says Mister Wads, 'but we'd best turn the boat around and check just in case.'

"So I tells Captain Ewan all of this, and he turns us back round, and wouldn't you know, that same Mister Wads suggested I use the big net to search in the shallows. He seemed to know exactly where to look. Must have a sixth sense or something.

"Very interesting," Willie whispers to you, his whiskers tickling your ear, "but we'll need to talk to each of our suspects."

He twitches his head over to port where Martha Green is hiding behind a pillar, arms wrapped around her body as she stares at Clyde's corpse.

You thank Biggie for his help and head toward her.

SUSPECT #1: The Secretary

Martha Green appears to be in her early twenties. She has short blonde hair and innocent doe eyes that are currently bright red. She blinks back tears as she sees you approach.

"I'm very sorry, I know I'm supposed to stay below deck, but I feel so sick. There's no way I can eat breakfast now. Poor Clyde!"

She pulls out a handkerchief from her pocket and wipes her nose.

You can't help but notice the yellow swan stitched onto the fabric.

"Oh that?" There's a flash of guilt in Martha's eyes when you inquire about the emblem. "It's Clyde's personal crest. He only puts it on his most precious items."

She begins sobbing loudly. You give her a minute to catch herself.

"That's a rather nice gift for him to give to his secretary," Willie mutters.

When Martha gathers her composure, you point this out to her.

"Yes, that's true," she admits. "But I wasn't just Clyde's secretary. I suppose there's no harm admitting it to you. Clyde and I were in love. He was going to leave his wife for me. He was going to tell her last night and then join me in my room. I knew something was wrong when he didn't show up. The old shrew must have poisoned him and then pushed his body over the side."

"Why poison?" you ask.

"Well because he'd have swam to safety otherwise," Martha points out. "The river's not that wide or that deep where we found him. At the very least, he would have screamed for help."

You mention the tie that was in his mouth, stopping him from shouting.

"Well that just confirms it!" Martha says. "That was Clyde's lucky tie! He loved it. Always wore it to important meetings. Who else would have had access to Clyde's things other than Veronica?"

Given the nature of their relationship, it seems likely that Martha would also have had access. When you point this out, she grows abashed.

"Yes that's true, but surely you don't think I had anything to do with this? I couldn't carry a dead body. Look at my arms, they're far too frail."

She gives you a sweet, watery smile before running off.

On your shoulder, Willie mutters, "Her arms look quite muscular to me. I don't think Martha is quite as weak as she'd like us to believe."

SUSPECT # 2: The Business Partner

"We should pay a visit to the wife next," Willie says, guiding you to the room. One of his great talents is knowing where everyone on the steamboat is staying.

You knock on the door. There's a groan from within, and a great deal of heavy steps as someone moves within. A moment later, a rather large man with disheveled salt-and-pepper hair and a thick mustache opens the door. You recognize him as Dennis Wads, Clyde's business partner.

For a moment, you begin to doubt Willie's talents. Has he brought you to the wrong suite?

"Denny Darling," a woman's voice calls from beyond, "Who's there?"

It's Veronica Mill. This is her room. But why is she referring to her husband's business partner with such familiarity?

"Just one of the crew," he says to her, before stepping outside into the narrow corridor. He scowls. "What do you want? Veronica's much too ill to be disturbed."

"The two of you seem quite close," you tell him.

He scowls, not bothering to hide his foul mood. "Yes, well, we've been carrying on an affair for the past five years, so I'd imagine we would. No sense hiding that now, is there? Clyde can hardly kill me from beyond the grave."

This is true, but the information does give Dennis Wads an obvious motive to murder his business partner. When you explain this, his scowl grows deeper.

"What are you talking about murder? Clyde got drunk and fell overboard! It was an accident. Hardly my fault he couldn't swim."

You mention the tie that was found in his mouth.

Dennis frowns for a moment. "Well, that is odd. But I'm certainly innocent! Believe me, even if I wanted Clyde dead, it would have been better for me if he'd lived another few weeks. He was about to retire and sell all his shares in our company to me! I'd have been in charge of everything. Now, I'm stuck with Henry as my partner. That privileged brat hasn't the faintest idea how to run a business. He's no head for numbers, or much else honestly. I tried to teach him cartography when he was a kid, that's a bit of a hobby of mine, but he could barely keep his eyes open. He wanted to fold the maps into paper cranes instead."

Dennis throws his hands up in the air, grumbling to himself. You're thinking what other information you might need from him when Veronica Mill opens her bedroom door and peeps into the hallway. There are dark circles under her bulging eyes and a few dark curls peep out from beneath a blue headscarf.

You notice the wing of a yellow swan poking out just above her forehead.

"Denny, please calm down. You're making my headache worse," she says, pressing her fingers to her temples. Her eyes narrow as she notices you.

You're worried that she's going to ask you to leave and refuse to speak, but instead, she turns to Dennis.

"Would you get me a glass of water, please? I need to take my pills."

Dennis looks at you. It seems he's about to protest, but Veronica gives him a look.

With a rather loud grumble, Dennis turns and stomps down the corridor.

Veronica winces and raises her hands to her ears. "He has the grace of a grizzly," she mutters, rubbing her forehead once more. Then she looks at you and asks, "Now, are you the crew member who found my husband's body?"

SUSPECT #3: The Wife

Veronica Mill invites you into her cabin as you explain the situation. She listens and nods. The murder of her husband doesn't seem to have affected her at all.

You notice that the cabin she and her husband shared is something of a mess. The scent of alcohol clings to the bedsheets. They must have snuck some on board. Captain Ewan is lax at checking for such things, not surprising given his own proclivities.

Clothing has been flung around the room. There's a single red heel by the door. Its companion is in the opposite corner, in a half-packed suitcase.

Veronica follows your gaze and quickly shuts the bag.

"Thank you for informing me about what's happened to my husband," she says. "I'll let the police know that they're to arrest Ms. Green when we dock."

Your eyes narrow.

"They were having an affair," Veronica explains, opening the drawer beside her bed and grabbing a bottle of pills. "You don't seem surprised. I suppose it was obvious. My husband has never been good at hiding his dalliances."

You watch as she struggles to open the bottle.

"They're always the same, girls with big innocent eyes who make him feel young. He invents stories of his own great achievements and talents. They fall for him, and he loses interest. It's quite unfortunate really. I was hoping this one might stick, and he'd finally let me leave." She sighs and holds out the bottle. "Can you help me with this?"

The pills appear to be painkillers. You twist the lid. It comes off easily. You don't pass it back just yet. Something Veronica said struck you as odd.

"You wanted a divorce?"

"For years," Veronica admits. "I love my husband, but I haven't been in love with him for a very long time. Ever since I started things with Dennis, I've been trying to leave, but Clyde wouldn't hear of it. He's a terrible cheat, but he wants the image of the perfect society wife on his arm. Every time I suggest it, he flies into a rage."

You glance around the messy room once more. "What happened last night, Ms. Mill?"

"We had dinner together in the ship's dining room with our son, Henry. Your chef made a delicious lobster chowder. Clyde loved it. He left a rather generous tip with our server, a small man with dark, shifty eyes. I do hope he shared it." She sighs before continuing.

"After dinner, I returned to the room while Clyde spoke to Henry. He had gifts for both of us, he said. I was expecting a pair of swan earrings or a new pendant. Instead, when he returned, he presented me with tickets for a boat to Europe. Apparently, Clyde wanted to retire and travel the world, with me at his side. The thought of having to play happy couple while he slept with every twenty-year-old that batted her eyes at him made me feel sick. I told him I knew about Martha and begged him to take her instead. He refused and said he was going to break up with her at once.

"That's when I finally came clean and confessed that I was having an affair of my own and no longer loved him. I wouldn't give him a name. He would've gone straight to Dennis' room and strangled him! But Clyde grew angry. That's when we started throwing things at one another. Eventually, he accused me of lying, declared he was going to end things with Martha, and vanished.

"I was so upset, I downed a bottle of gin and blacked out. Dennis woke me this morning with the news. Obviously, Martha didn't take the break-up well."

She holds out her hand for her pill bottle.

You thank her for the information and pass it back. However, before you can leave, there's a knock on the door.

The very person you were hoping to see enters.

. . .

SUSPECT #4: The Son

Henry Mill is a slender man with tousled good-looks. He's dressed in a stylish cotton suit with soft-toed slippers better suited for a bedroom than a steamboat. He steps into the room without a sound, a concerned frown on his face as his eyes go from you to his mother.

There's a glass of water in his hand.

"I thought you might need this," he says, passing it to Veronica.

"You are a sweetheart, Henry," she says, smiling at her son as she accepts the glass. "I'd just sent Dennis to get some." She takes her pills, hand trembling from the weight of the glass.

"I know," Henry says. "I saw him in the dining area and offered to bring you the water instead. Your husband just died. People might get the wrong impression if they see another man comforting you so soon."

From the pointed look, it's obvious that Henry at least suspects that his mother and Dennis Wads are having an affair.

Veronica sighs, closes her eyes, and lies on her bed. "Not now, Henry, please. My husband was just murdered. Save your lectures. I just want a moment of peace."

At Veronica's insistence, you and Henry both leave.

He begins to walk back toward the dining room in search of Dennis Wads.

You follow.

"Don't you have a job that you ought to be doing now?" Henry asks, glancing back at you from the corner of his eye. His tone is laced with condescension.

You ignore it and continue to walk alongside him.

A small voice whispers in your ear, "Ask him about what happened last night with his father."

You do.

A look of anger flashes across Henry's eyes. "What business is it of yours? We spoke about a personal matter, and then he returned to his cabin. At least, as far as I know."

Veronica also mentioned a gift. You press harder until Henry stops before the dining room door and turns to you with a frown.

"My father wanted to inform me that he was retiring and selling his shares in the company to Dennis. For a pittance, really, but he wasn't asking my opinion. He just wanted me to know that he still loved me and offered to help find me a job. The gift you're so concerned about was this." He pulls a handkerchief from his pocket and presents it to you.

It's black with gold roses embroidered around the edges. The soft, silky fabric is clean and new. You're no expert, but it feels expensive.

Henry snatches it back from you, folds it, and returns it to his pocket.

"Now, please, leave us all in peace," he says and disappears into the kitchen.

A moment later, the whistle signals that the steamboat is approaching land. As first mate, you have duties to attend to on deck. There's no time left to question the suspects further.

"Perfect timing," Willie says. "Now that we've spoken to all the suspects, it's obvious who the murderer is. Make sure you tell the police right away once we've docked!"

It's your job to tell the police who to arrest.

Your Answer

WHO KILLED CLYDE MILL?

1. Martha Green, the secretary
2. Dennis Wads, the business partner
3. Veronica Mill, the wife
4. Henry Mill, the son

If you need a hint, turn to the back of this book.
If you know the culprit, turn the page for the solution.

The Solution

Answer: Henry Mill

YOU DISCUSS the matter with Willie, and when the police arrive, you instruct them to arrest Henry Mill.

Henry protests. "Why would I have killed my father?"

The reason is obvious.

"Money," you explain to everyone gathered on the dock. "Clyde wanted to sell his business shares and spend the money traveling through Europe. Henry would have lost most of his inheritance.

"When Clyde informed him of his decision, he gave his son a gift— his very own tie, which had served him well in his own business. Henry was furious. He waited until later that night, and when he saw his father leave his room, he snuck up on him. Henry knew his father couldn't swim, so he shoved the tie into Clyde's mouth to block his cries, then pushed him overboard."

Just your word might not be enough for the police, but Henry's eyes grow wide and nervous as he listens. When you finish, he tries to make a run for it.

One of the policemen catches him, grabs his wrists and marches him away. Another takes the tie, placing it in a bag.

"Chances are, this tie will have some evidence that Henry Mill is the killer," the officer says, and he thanks you for your help.

Martha is in tears as she leaves the steamboat. Veronica is as pale as a sheet, unable to walk without Dennis' support.

Biggie comes up beside you, watching the three innocent suspects as they depart. "How'd you know it wasn't any of them?" he asks.

"Denis Wads is too loud. You'd have heard him moving up on the deck and woken up if he was the killer. As a hobby cartographer, he'd also have known to throw the body where it couldn't be found. On top of all that, he had the weakest motive. He wanted Clyde's business shares.

Veronica Mill is too weak. She struggled to open a bottle of pills or hold a full glass of water. There's no way she could have shoved a tie into her husband's mouth or pushed him over a steamboat.

Martha Green might be strong enough to have committed the murder, and if Clyde had broken up with her that night, she'd have a good motive. But Martha never knew that Clyde couldn't swim. If she'd wanted to kill him, she'd have used another approach."

Biggie purses his lips. For a moment, you think he'll compliment your detective skills.

Instead, he saunters off, muttering, "Still think it's a pity we couldn't keep that tie."

Case #3: The Speakeasy Shooting

IT'S your second week as first mate on the SS Wilkinshire, and you finally have a day off. The steamboat is docked at Brackwell Port, a small riverside town with a seedy underbelly.

You decide to go into town to stretch your legs. Willie comes with you, riding on your shoulder. He's hoping for a piece of cheese.

"I've heard wonderful things about parmesan," he says, rubbing his hands together in delight. "Think you could buy me a little? I don't eat much."

That's not quite true. You've been sharing your meals with your new mouse friend the past couple weeks. He puts away more than you'd expect, given his size.

But, you've gotten your first set of wages. There's money in your pocket. Why not buy him a treat?

"Where's the cheesemonger?" you ask.

He points you down a side street.

As you're walking toward the cheese seller, a familiar voice calls your name.

You turn and see Joe Steely, the large chef of the SS Wilkinshire, running toward you.

"Thought it was you," he says, stopping a few feet away to catch his breath. "I need your help. I think there's been a murder."

* * *

Joe takes you to a large brick building. The wooden door to the foyer swings open without issue, and the two of you walk down a long flight of stairs into a candle-lit basement.

Willie peeps out from behind your collar. You can feel his ears brushing against the edge of your jaw.

You arrive in a large speakeasy. There are tables and chairs arranged throughout the room, and a long black bar on one side. There are two glasses near the sink, each with a dribble of clear liquid within. There's lip smudges around the rims, suggesting these were recently used.

"I came in to get a drink. The Ginger Lily has the best rum of anywhere within 20 miles. Instead, I found him behind the bar," Joe explains, gesturing for you to go and look.

A fair-haired man lies face-down on the floor. There's a pool of blood around his stomach, and a hole in his white shirt suggests that he was shot by a gun. A gold watch glitters on his left wrist. The arm has been bent into an awkward angle. His bones must have broken when he fell. Judging from the location of the wound, he probably wasn't aware of the pain for long, if at all.

"That's Ray Slick," Joe tells you. "He runs The Ginger Lily, or used to."

Willie climbs over your collar and scurries down your arm, sniffing the air.

Joe doesn't seem to notice the mouse investigating.

You turn to your crew member. "Why'd you ask me to come? Shouldn't you call the police?"

"Already did. Gave a kid on the street a penny and

sent him running. They should be here soon. But then I saw you, and I remembered what a good job you'd done when Mr. Mill drowned. I thought you might be able to help."

You don't see how, but before you can apologize and continue on your mission to purchase parmesan, Willie squeaks.

Joe's brow knots together as he tries to figure out where the noise originated.

You look around and see that Willie has climbed up onto the bar. He's standing on his back paws and waving at you from beside a large record player.

You hurry toward him, blocking him from Joe's sight.

"I think I've found something," Willie says. With his tail, he points to something beside him.

At first, you think he means the record sleeve. It's plain white, the phrase Bird Song scrawled across the top in a man's slanted writing. Then his little paws tug at the corner of something flat beneath. He presents it to you before scurrying off again.

Joe approaches, peering over your shoulder as you unfold a piece of paper.

It's a note, written with a typewriter.

Time's up, Slick. I've been more than patient. Either you give me what I'm owed, or I'll take it myself.

Unfortunately, there's no signature.

Joe bends down and search's Ray Slick's pockets. "Empty," he says. "You suppose the killer was after money?"

You consider this as you look at the corpse. It's possible, but none of this is much to go on.

From the corner of your eye, you spot Willie jumping up and down, a little blur of yellow and gray.

What's he found this time?

You slide over to the other side of the bar where Willie has managed to pull open a drawer with his tail. There's a small blue ledger within.

You open it to reveal Ray Slick's record book. He kept a list of his various debts. It seems he had a tendency to borrow.

There's a lot of names, but only four loans jump out as significant enough to account for a murder:

Duncan Devilish, Ray's landlord. The speakeasy owner hadn't paid him in almost six months.

Lydia Lightfinger, labeled only as a business associate. She'd extended a small loan that was accruing unpaid interest.

Horace Bore, police officer. Several small figures beside his name add up to a significant sum.

Janice Bird, singer. A note in the ledger suggests she was low on Ray's priority list.

Willie winks at you before scurrying up your arm and back onto your shoulder. "I think we have our suspects."

SUSPECT #1: The Police Officer

As you're studying the names in the ledger, you hear a set of loud footsteps pounding down the stairs.

Two police officers enter the speakeasy. They're both in shiny blue uniforms, guns on their hips.

One is small and old with a wispy moustache. The other is a blond, shaped like a sphere. His two chins wobble as he approaches. You can't help but notice that the silver tag on his uniform reads: Horace Bore.

"Well, well, well. Whaddya think happened here?" Horace says, scratching beneath his chins. "Was Ray Slick running a speakeasy?" He widens his eyes in exaggerated shock. "He must've gotten himself into trouble running with that crowd!"

He looks to his partner for support.

The older man snorts, and the hair trembles on his moustache. "Don't pretend you didn't know. I wasn't born yesterday, Horace." He turns to you and Joe. "Who was it that found the body?"

The older policeman takes Joe aside. Horace slips on a pair of gloves and bends down to examine the corpse. His hands go straight to Ray's watch. He fumbles with the clasp for a moment before he notices you watching him.

Horace stares up at you, eyes defiant. "Don't go getting the wrong impression. I'm doing essential police work, collecting evidence."

When you don't respond, he takes your silence for accusation.

Horace's lips turn into a scowl, disappearing into the folds of his cheeks. "You're quite a bold one to stick around a speakeasy like this. I ought to arrest you for drinking. Though I suppose I might be persuaded to look the other way."

Is he threatening you?

"Funny," you say, "I think you're the one who seems suspicious here. Not me." You show him Ray's record book.

"Give me that," Horace growls, trying to grab it from you as he stands. His balance is off, and instead, he wobbles backward and falls against the bar. "What're you trying to insinuate? I'm an upstanding member of the community! Those monthly payments from Ray were a thanks for my protecting the neighborhood. He wasn't bribing me to look the other way."

You exchange a look with the mouse on your shoulder.

Horace Bore is not the brightest. Somehow, his lies are as incriminating as the truth.

But you're not concerned about bribes.

"When was the last time you saw Ray Slick?" you ask Horace.

A worried expression comes over his face. He glances across the room to where his partner is still talking to Joe, then leans closer to you.

"Listen," Horace whispers. "Maybe I paid Ray a visit this morning around ten o'clock to inquire about his late payment with my, ah, gifts. But he was alive when I left."

Before you realize what's happening, Horace's hand darts toward you, and he tears the book from your hand. He's faster than you'd expected given his size.

"Now let's see. Ah ha!" Horace shouts, studying the ledger. He slaps a stubby finger on one of the names. "Lydia Lightfinger! She's a criminal if I ever met one. Runs a serious bootlegging operation. She's the one who supplied all the alcohol to this place, though it looks like Ray's been buying on credit for a while. Lydia is wealthy as sin."

Perhaps thinking he needs to prove it to you, Horace stoops and points to the gold watch on Ray's wrist. "She gives one of these to everyone she has business dealings with as a gift. Real gold! And she don't bat an eye at it. Yet she refuses to give an honest cop like me a dime. She's who you should be investigating!"

You raise your eyebrows at him. "Shouldn't you investigate her? You're the policeman."

"Are you insane? I can't just march up to Lydia's mansion and start asking questions. She's got a team of lawyers. Plus, she hates my guts for trying to arrest her for not contributing to my retirement fund. She might shoot me on sight. And she's quick with her gun while I'm the slowest shot there is."

He reaches toward his holster with exaggerated slug-gishness.

Then, with a big grin, he turns toward his partner, waving the ledger in the air. "Look what I found, Turner! You'll have to thank me for finding the key to solving this thing."

"Come on," Willie whispers from your shoulder. "I don't

think we're going to get much more from him. We should pay Lydia Lightfinger a visit."

SUSPECT #2: The Bootlegger

Horace wasn't exaggerating about Lydia Lightfinger's wealth.

After asking directions from the townspeople of Brackwell, you and Willie follow the river about a mile out of town and arrive at a massive manor.

It's protected by a large fence.

You can't see how you'll get in to speak with anyone.

Crack! Crack! Crack!

Those are three gunshots. You jump, alert to your surroundings. But you don't see casings anywhere close to you.

"Look over there," Willie whispers, standing and balancing on his back legs to peer over your collar. "In the corner of the property."

You follow his instructions and see a slender woman with a short red ponytail standing ten feet from a thick wooden board with a paper target stuck in the center. A silver revolver shines in her hand. She blows the top, spins it around, and returns it to the holster at her hip.

"That must be Lydia," Willie says. "We need to talk to her."

A lump rises in your throat as your gaze goes to the revolver. But you take a deep breath and step forward, calling her name.

She tilts her head at the sound and steps forward. As she approaches, you get a better look at her face. She has pale lips and light eyes. Her lashes are difficult to see in the sunlight, and there's a splattering of freckles over her cheeks. Her expression is curious, not unkind. But her hand hovers near her gun. "I seem to be at a disadvantage. You know my name, and I don't know yours."

You introduce yourself. Then you tell her about Ray Slick's murder.

"Not surprising," she says. "Ray's been ignoring his debts for almost half a year and digging himself into a financial pit. He was never going to make enough to recover his losses. Someone must have found a different way for him to pay. What's that to do with me?"

"He owed you a lot of money."

"True," she admits. "So his death is my loss too. He doesn't have a wife or any children to repay me. It's a pity. I'm not running a charity."

Perhaps you ought to be, you think, glancing at the sprawling manor behind her once more. "What did Ray owe you money for?"

"Oh you know, this and that." She bats her eyes. If she's trying to look innocent, the gun at her hip is ruining it. "Who told you to come speak to me about this anyway? You're not with the Brackwell police."

You shake your head. "Just a curious bystander. But Horace Bore mentioned you."

Lydia's jaw clenches at the name. "Of course he did. The pig. He's got it out for me. Let me show you something."

She holds up a finger, asking for a moment as she goes toward the wooden board she's just shot. Lydia pulls the piece of paper from it and passes it to you through the fence.

You glance down and read.

Police Report: Horace Bore

Incident: Lydia Litefinger was seen loytering near the port with two nown dejenerates. When aproached, Litefinger—

The rest of the report has been torn up by gunshot. It's impossible to read.

"He submitted two dozen of those," Lydia informs you. "Luckily, the chief of police is an old friend of my father's. He sent me Horace's ridiculous reports so I could have a laugh. Somehow the poor fool has got it in his head that I'm the head of a criminal organization, who ought to be paying him to turn the other way. It's utterly absurd. I fully intend to have him fired in the most humiliating way possible. I'm a woman trying to run a successful business. I can't tolerate disrespect from pathetic little men."

You can hear the fury in her voice at the perceived slight. It seems safer to avoid the topic of Horace.

"What business are you in, Ms. Lightfinger?" you ask instead.

"Shipping and distribution. My father established the company. He paid for my education in Canada so that I'd be properly equipped to take it over after his passing. Thanks to him, I'm well-versed in business and have all the right connections."

A smile plays on her lips as she waits for your response. She's taunting you. Everything she's admitted hints heavily towards a massive bootlegging operation, bringing the alcohol over from Canada and transporting it down the river.

But Lydia is wealthy. She knows there's nothing you can do to touch her. And, having seen the way she was firing at Horace's report, you don't want to get on her bad side either.

You turn to leave.

She reaches through the fence and grabs your hand before you can.

"Wait," she says. "If you're looking for the killer, you should talk to Ray's landlord, Duncan Devilish. He's an old man with a horrible temper. The last time I saw Ray was a few days ago. He came to me, begging me to extend his credit, and mentioned that Duncan was threatening to evict him. I doubt Ray planned to go peacefully."

You thank her for her help, and leave the estate, making your way back toward town. The gunshots echo again as Lydia resumes her target practice.

"Interesting woman," Willie whispers, peering at her over your shoulder as you walk. "Definitely a bootlegger."

SUSPECT #3: The Landlord

Before visiting Duncan Devilish, you ask around and learn a bit about the landlord. After Lydia, he's the wealthiest person in Brackwell, owning all of the houses on the street where Ray Slick operated his speakeasy.

Despite all his property, Duncan is seldom in Brackwell, preferring to stay on his country estate, a half day's drive from the town.

"Do you think it's just a coincidence that he'd be here on the day Ray gets murdered?" Willie asks, making himself comfortable on your shoulder as you approach the door.

It's a good question. You're not certain of the answer.

Duncan Devilish is staying on the bottom floor of one of his many apartment buildings.

You knock twice.

A few moments later, a grizzled old man with leathery skin and calloused hands pulls the door open. His eyes narrow, and he scowls at you. "You're not one of my tenants."

Very astute.

"You must be Duncan Devilish," you say, offering your hand in greeting. You tell him your name and explain why you're here.

"Ray is dead, you say?" Duncan rubs the stubble on his chin. "I should've suspected. I heard him arguing with that policeman—what's his name?—Bore, yesterday morning. Then that beautiful singer stopped by and there was the gunshot."

This is a lot of new information. You wonder if you ought to take a note.

"Let me guess," Duncan continues. "You want to rent his place now that it's free. Smart of you to get in quick. It's one of my nicer houses given the basement. Well, come on in. We can draw up a contract from now."

You do miss living on land, but given your current situation, it's out of the question. Plus, you've grown fond of Willie, and you're not sure the mouse would want to live anywhere other than his beloved steamboat.

But if you explain this to Duncan, he might not be as eager to welcome you into his apartment. So you keep your mouth shut and follow him in.

He leads you into a small sitting area. It's utilitarian, designed for practicality instead of comfort. There are no paintings or decorations, only three chairs, a sturdy wooden table and a push cart full of newspapers and pens.

Duncan sits, and the legs of his pants rise.

"He has a gun strapped to his ankle," Willie whispers.

You spot it just before Duncan leans forward, and his pants drop.

"It must be a relief for you to be able to find a new tenant," you say, trying to get comfortable on the cushionless wooden seat. "I gather Ray wasn't very good about paying his rent."

"Terrible. Owed me almost six months," he admits. He grabs a pen and wags it at you. "But don't think I just accept that from my tenants. Ray and I had already agreed that if he couldn't find the money, he was going to give me his watch. It was quite valuable. Real gold, I understand. I have the contract here."

Duncan searches in his papers and passes one to you. It's a handwritten contract. Ray Slick's signature is at the bottom. You see mention of a watch, but the landlord takes it back from you before you can read all the details.

"Suppose it's null and void now that Ray's dead," Duncan says. "But enough about him. Let's talk about what you'll need." The landlord wastes no time providing you with the details. He runs through the rent price, security deposit, and where to take the garbage.

You listen, nodding along, waiting for an opportunity to return to the topic of Ray's death.

Duncan has a pen in one hand and a book open on the tray before him. He pauses to write every few seconds.

You realize that he's drawing up a contract based on everything you're agreeing to.

Suddenly, you feel guilty for misleading him.

You clear your throat and blurt out the first thing that comes to you. "I'm afraid I really need to know more about Ray's death before I can commit to a long-term rental."

Duncan stops writing and frowns. "Concerns about the safety of the area?"

You don't respond, but he continues as if you've agreed.

"I wouldn't let it worry you too much. You didn't hear this from me, but Ray was running a speakeasy in his basement. He swore it was going to turn a profit thanks to his incredible moonshine, but he got himself involved with the wrong crowd."

You seize the opportunity to return to your intended line of questioning. "Did you say a policeman visited him earlier today?"

Duncan nods. "I saw when Horace Bore went in early this morning. He's a real pain, the type that wanted to be a criminal but wasn't smart enough, so he went into law enforcement to bully everyone that way instead. I heard he was threatening to arrest Ray if he didn't pay up. Maybe he decided to kill him instead."

"What about the singer?"

An odd expression passes over Duncan's face. His lips press together, and his brow lowers. You get the impression that he doesn't want to tell you the next bit. "Janice Bird. I didn't see her go in, but I'd recognize her voice anywhere. I was passing by Ray's place just before midday when I heard her in there with him. The gunshot went off a few moments later. But I'm sure it wasn't her. She's a beautiful girl with the voice of an angel, certainly not a killer."

"I think we'll need to confirm that for ourselves," Willie whispers.

SUSPECT # 4: The Singer

You explain to Duncan that you need to speak to Janice yourself before you'll feel comfortable renting. He seems perplexed by this but tells you where to find her.

Janice Bird is renting a room at a hotel near the docks, singing in the lobby as payment for her stay.

You catch the end of her performance as you arrive.

Janice is wearing a tight red dress that leaves little to the imagination. Dark curls cascade over one of her shoulders. Her face is beautiful, but the real star is her voice. She's hitting notes that you didn't know a human was capable of singing.

The crowd in the lobby applauds. She curtsies, blows a few kisses, and disappears into the elevator. Willie leaps from your shoulder and darts across the floor, managing to slip in before the doors close.

A guard blocks anyone else from following.

You watch the numbers light up on the sign as the elevator rises. It stops at the seventh floor.

Why couldn't it have been the second?

You sigh as you head toward the stairs and start your climb.

When you reach the seventh floor, Willie is waiting for you.

"What took you so long? She's staying in the room on the left, two doors down." He hops onto your shoe, sitting on it for a moment before climbing back to your shoulder.

You gather your breath and knock on the door.

"Oh good, you're early this time. I hope you remembered to take the peas out of my broth or—" Janice Bird opens the door. At the sight of you, her eyes grow wide and she stops speaking.

Your eyebrows rise.

Gone is the beautiful woman from before. In her place is a rather ordinary blonde with her thin hair clipped on the top of her head. Dark smudges around her eyes suggest that she's in the middle of removing her makeup.

"A fan!" Janice squeaks, covers her face with her hands, and retreats into her room.

She doesn't close the door, so you follow.

Janice has gone into the cramped bedroom to sit before a large vanity. One hand reapplies her red lipstick while the other powders her face. There's a brown wig with curls on a bust beside her.

"Just a moment," she says, not realizing that you're standing in the doorway.

You consider the rest of the room. It's clear no one has been in to clean today. The sheets are unmade and discarded tissues lie scattered on the floor. There's an empty plate and a glass rimmed with lipstick on the bedside table. Something silver pokes out from beneath the pillow.

Janice places her wig on her head and turns toward you, all nervous smiles and rushed makeup. "So, have you come for an autograph? I really don't approve of fans following me like this, you know."

Judging from her giggle, this isn't true.

Willie sneaks out from your sleeve and climbs onto the bed to investigate beneath the pillow.

In the meantime, Janice is busy signing a piece of paper. She presses her lips to it and passes it to you. "I mark everything I write with a kiss," she informs you.

You slip it into your pocket, but don't waste time. "I heard you visited Ray Slick earlier today."

Janice deflates as she realizes that you're not a fan seeking an autograph. With a sigh, she removes her wig and scratches her scalp. "I don't know who gave you that information, but it's nonsense. I've been in the room all morning. A good singer needs beauty sleep. I try to avoid waking before noon."

From the corner of your eye, you see Willie pointing frantically to the silver item beneath the pillow.

You creep closer.

"What're you—" Janice starts to object as your hand reaches for the hidden object. "Careful!"

The glint of silver is the blade of a large knife. You realize just in time and avoid grabbing it. That was close: you could've sliced open your wrist. Instead, you lift the pillow and take it by the hilt.

Willie sneaks up your other arm.

"Stop! Don't hurt me! I'll call the guard," Janice says, her voice shaking as she attempts to retreat from her own room.

You realize that she's afraid. You set the blade down

quickly. "I only want to ask a few questions. Why have you got such a thing under your pillow?"

Janice relaxes now that you're not brandishing a weapon. She presses a hand to her chest and leans against the vanity.

"For protection obviously. A lot of talented people attract stalkers. I need to be prepared."

Her red lips curve into a smile. You get the impression that Janice wants to be stalked.

"When was the last time you spoke to Ray Slick?"

"That jerk?" Janice snorts and plops back into her chair. She grabs a tissue and begins cleaning her hastily powdered face. "I only came back to this town because he swore he'd have my money by now. But instead, he shows up a few days ago trying to convince me that he got me this job, so we ought to be even. Utterly ridiculous! They're barely paying beyond food and board. And, do you want to hear the worst of it? Ray wanted me to come back to his greasy place and sing another night for free! Said if he didn't get more money, his life was at risk. As if he couldn't just sell that fancy watch of his for the money. Pah!"

"Did he say who was threatening him?"

"No, but he was probably just exaggerating. Now, I've had enough of talking about Ray Slick. Leave me alone before I scream for the guard."

* * *

You hurry out of the hotel and onto the street.

Willie shuffles so that he's sitting more comfortably on your shoulder.

"Well, now that this is all sorted, let's inform the police about the identity of the murderer and then reward ourselves with some cheese," he says. "It's quite clear which one of our suspects is guilty."

Your Answer

WHO MURDERED RAY SLICK?

1. Horace Bore, the policeman
2. Lydia Lightfinger, the bootlegger
3. Duncan Devilish, the landlord
4. Janice Bird, the singer

If you need a hint, turn to the back of this book.
If you know the culprit, turn the page for the solution.

The Solution

Answer: Lydia Lightfinger

WHEN YOU ARRIVE at the police station, you spot Turner, the old officer with the wispy moustache sitting at his desk. Joe is with him, giving an official statement about how he found the body.

You walk up to them, slap your palms on the desk, and announce, "I've solved it. Ray Slick was murdered by Lydia Lightfinger."

They stop talking.

"How're you so confident?" Turner asks. "Do you have any evidence?"

Having discussed the case with Willie, you know how to explain.

"Ray wasn't robbed. His pockets were empty because he didn't have money, but his real treasure, his gold watch, was still on his wrist. If the murderer wanted their money, they could have stolen the watch and recouped their losses. The fact that they left it behind shows that this wasn't about money. It was personal. Lydia didn't like that Ray was refusing to pay her back. She murdered him to prove that she won't tolerate late payments when it comes to her business.

"Ray had already agreed to give his landlord the watch as payment if he couldn't make rent, so Duncan Devilish had little motive.

"The first thing Horace Bore did when he investigated the body was search the pockets. If he was the killer, he'd already have known they were empty. Plus, he'd definitely have stolen the watch.

"Although Duncan thought he heard Janice's voice in the speakeasy when Ray was killed, this was most likely one of her records. Janice doesn't own a gun and also didn't seem aware that Ray was dead.

On top of all that, there's the threatening note. Duncan writes all his information by hand, Horace can't spell, and Janice signs hers with a kiss. Lydia is educated and wealthy enough to own a typewriter, so she's the only plausible culprit."

Officer Turner looks shocked.

Joe grins. "Told you our first mate has a knack for these things."

You avoid looking at the mouse hiding behind your collar.

"Thanks, Joe," you say, nodding your head. You turn, heading out of the police station.

"Where are you going?" Turner calls after you. "Don't you want to explain all that to the chief?"

Definitely not since you already know he's in Lydia's pocket. She won't be arrested. But at least you and Willie cracked the case.

A victorious smile spreads across your face, and you shout back, "I'm going to buy some cheese!"

Case #4: The Stolen Silverware

YOU'RE TAKING A WELL-DESERVED break in your cabin as the SS Wilkinshire crew take a day off at your current whistlestop. There's a book open on your bed. You turn the pages.

Willie sits near your elbow, reading over your shoulder. It's a habit you've tried to break, but the mouse won't listen. He says that he has no choice but to read that way. He's too small to turn the pages otherwise.

You hear a shout echo through the narrow passageway and into your room.

"Sounds like it's coming from the kitchen," Willie says. "Should we check it out?"

You're less curious than the mouse. But the shout is followed by the clangs of drawers slamming and objects being tossed onto the floor. Soon, you can hear your crewmates arguing.

You walk to the kitchen with Willie riding in the pocket of your shirt, his nose and eyes peeping out.

You open the door. Your eyebrows arch.

The kitchen is a mess. Cutlery litters the floor. Joe and Captain Ewan are arguing in the center of the kitchen.

"You've probably lost it," the Captain says, waving his hands at the chef.

Joe's broad jaw clenches into a scowl. He waves his arm at the mess. "I've been searching since midday. They're not here. You'll have to buy new ones!"

"Absolutely not. I've told you—" The Captain stops, suddenly noticing you. He coughs and turns toward you with an embarrassed look. "Ah, if it isn't my finest first mate. I'm sorry you've walked in and found us like this. I'm afraid that Joe has misplaced the ship's silverware."

"Someone's taken it," Joe says. "Maybe one of the guests."

"I used some just this morning with my breakfast," Captain Ewan says, chuckling and wagging his finger at the chef. "No one's on the ship but us. So you'll have to come up with a better excuse than that."

Willie tugs on the fabric of your shirt. You know exactly what the mouse wants.

You sigh. So much for spending a quiet hour with a book before arriving at the next port.

"Leave it to me," you tell the Captain and the chef. "I'll find who's taken the missing silverware."

SUSPECT #1: Joe

You convince Captain Ewan to leave the kitchen while you talk to the chef. Joe mutters to himself as he puts the scattered cutlery, none of which is the good silverware, back in the drawers.

"I can tell you who did this," he says. "It was Captain

Ewan himself! Don't let him fool you. I saw him heading toward the kitchens after I left. I've been complaining to him about how terrible the silverware is for ages. If I know him, this is his way of teaching me a lesson. Bet he thinks I'll say that bad silverware is better than no silverware."

You write down the crucial bit of information hidden in his rant. Given what you heard prior, it seems evident that the silverware went missing at some point this morning. You question Joe about his whereabouts.

He throws his hands up in frustration. "I was in my cabin when the silverware vanished. After making breakfast, I was tired. I went to lie down and work on a handkerchief I'm embroidering. I can't be in the kitchen all the time. It's not a crime to need a break!"

After that, he shoos you from the kitchen.

SUSPECT #2: Captain Ewan

The Captain is waiting to talk to you as soon as you're through the door. He launches into an accusation.

"Joe is one who took the silverware! He's been complaining about it since he started working here. He probably assumed that if he chucked it into the harbor, I'd have to buy him a new set. I'll bet, if you go diving, you'll find all of it at the bottom of the river."

You figure this is all he needs to tell you, but before you can go to one of the other crew members, Captain Ewan grabs your arm and pulls you back.

"There's one more thing," he says. "If you're going to bother investigating the others, don't worry about Gertie. It definitely wasn't her. She wasn't on the ship this morning. I sent her into town to run some errands."

SUSPECT #3: Estelle

You find Estelle in one of the guest cabins, mopping the floor. She doesn't bother stopping while you explain the situation with the missing silverware.

"Well, it wasn't me," she says finally. "I haven't even cleaned the kitchen yet today. And truthfully, when I do, I never remember to think about the silverware."

You press for more information about her whereabouts, she grows annoyed.

"I spent the morning alone cleaning the crews' cabins just like I always do. Not that any of you ever say thank you! I suppose you think clean sheets just magically appear on your bed. I'd have someone vouch for me, but no one else came down there after breakfast."

SUSPECT #4: Biggie

You find Biggie lying on the deck, a hat over his head to block the sun. For a moment, you think he's sleeping, but he flies up at once at the sound of your footsteps.

He's annoyed when he realizes that it's you who's disturbed his sleep.

You explain that the silverware is missing and vanished at

some point between breakfast and midday and ask if he has any information.

Biggie shakes his head. "I was busy all morning cleaning the boilers. Don't know why it's always my job to check on them. I'm absolutely exhausted! Joe better make me two servings today!"

It's a bit annoying that no one seems to be able to validate anyone else's alibi. You mention this, and Biggie thinks for a moment, a shifty look in his eyes.

"I can tell you that it wasn't Captain Ewan," he says. "He was up on the quarterdeck patrolling this morning."

SUSPECT #5: Gertie

Gertie comes up onto the deck and spots you as you're leaving Biggie.

"He's definitely lying about working on the boiler," she tells you. "I saw him in those same clothes when I left this morning, and they're still clean."

That's interesting, assuming Gertie is telling the truth.

You tell her about the incident with the silverware and ask if she's any idea what could have happened.

She's quick to defend herself. "It wasn't me. I was in the market purchasing fresh supplies just like Captain Ewan instructed."

Who stole the silverware?

"That was quite an interesting set of interviews," Willie says, as you return to your room. He climbs out of your pocket and onto your bed, making himself comfortable on your pillow as he explains. "Everyone gave you two pieces of information, but only one of them told the truth both times."

Your eyebrows furrow as you look at the mouse, tugging at his bright yellow fishing jacket. "How do you know that?"

"I've been on this boat long enough to know when the crew are lying or telling the truth."

"So you know who stole the silverware!"

"I do," Willie says. His whiskers twitch as he turns to you. "The thief is the only person who lied both times they spoke."

Willie has given you a clue to help you solve the mystery.

Your Answer

WHO STOLE THE SILVERWARE?

1. Joe
2. Captain Ewan
3. Estelle
4. Biggie
5. Gertie

If you need a hint, turn to the back of this book.
If you know the culprit, turn the page for the solution.

The Solution

Answer: Estelle

YOU'VE FIGURED IT OUT. You race to find Captain Ewan. He's in the dining room with both Gertie and Estelle.

"I know who took the silverware," you say. "It was her!"

You point to Estelle.

Thanks to Willie's assistance and your own logical reasoning, you realized that if only one person told the truth both times, the only person who could have lied twice is Estelle.

"If you'd been in our cabins cleaning this whole morning, you'd have known that Joe was there too," you explain. "He was working on his embroidery. But you were in the kitchen, taking the silverware. I'll bet you've hidden it somewhere with your cleaning supplies."

Gertie gasps. Captain Ewan's cheeks puff out. He turns to the cleaner. "Is this true, Estelle?"

You expect her to deny it, but instead, she nods her head.

"I did take the silverware," she explains. "But only because I was going to clean it and put it back as a nice surprise for Joe.

I didn't think anyone would notice. We never use it unless there's someone fancy on board."

She gives you a sour look before turning to bat her eyes at the Captain.

You're not convinced that's the truth at all.

But Captain Ewan buys it at once. "That's the sort of spirit I like to see from my crew! We're all one big family here on the SS Wilkinshire, aren't we?" He grins and pulls both girls into a hug.

Over Captain Ewan's shoulder, Estelle sticks her tongue out at you.

Terribly rude!

But at least you solved the case and can return to your book.

Captain Ewan steps forward and puts his arm around your shoulder dragging you with him as he leaves the dining room. "Come on then," he says. "I think it's time we head off."

You sigh. Sometimes, there's no reward for a mystery solved.

The Extended Solution

IF JOE HAD TOLD the truth both times, Captain Ewan would be guilty. But that would mean Captain Ewan is telling the truth when he says that Gertie is innocent.

If Captain Ewan told the truth both times, either Biggie or Gertie would also have needed to tell the truth twice.

If Estelle told the truth twice, Joe would be lying about being in the cabin and therefore telling the truth about Captain Ewan. However, that doesn't work because the Captain said that Gertie was innocent, which must be true if he's the culprit.

Whether it's Biggie or Gertie that's telling the truth, Estelle is the only person who could have lied twice.

Willie confirms this by writing a T, for truth, and an L, for lie, by each statement you've recorded in your notes.

JOE:

I was in my cabin when the silverware vanished. - T

It was Captain Ewan who took it. - L

CAPTAIN EWAN:

Joe is one who took the silverware. - L
It definitely wasn't Gertie. - T

ESTELLE:

It wasn't me. - L

I spent the morning alone cleaning the cabins. I was the only one there. - L

BIGGIE:

I was busy all morning cleaning the boilers. - L

It wasn't Captain Ewan. He was up on the quarterdeck patrolling this morning. - T

GERTIE:

Biggie is lying about working on the boilers. - T

It wasn't me. - T

Case #5: A Murder Most Holy

~

YOUR NEXT WHISTLESTOP IS BRIGHTVILLE, a growing city on the edge of the river.

Estelle has a son who lives here now, and she's familiar with the area. After you caught her stealing the silverware, she's been snappish and cold, refusing to follow your directions and only listening to the captain.

In an attempt to better the relationship between you and Estelle, Captain Ewan decides to send you into the city together to purchase the supplies.

You walk down the broad, bustling main street, stopping in at a variety of different shops. Unknown to the cleaner, Willie is hiding in your pocket. You see his nose peep out to sniff the air as you step into the grocers.

Estelle argues with you over which supplies are best, trying to put vegetables you don't want into your hands.

After you refuse to purchase a pair of already soft tomatoes, she gets annoyed. "Listen to me," she says, holding the tomatoes as though she wants to throw them at your head. "Just because you're First Mate doesn't mean anything. I've been alive longer than you. I've spent more time on that ship than you. I know this city better than you."

"That's true," you say quickly, trying to ease the tension and avoid having a tomato splattered on your head. "Tell me about the city."

Estelle sniffs. "Brightville is nothing like what visitors think. All you see is the shiny storefronts and the big churches. There is a sizable religious movement growing in the city. But there's a dark side to Brightville too."

A dangerous glint comes into Estelle's eyes. She grabs your arm, pulling you out of the grocer's before you can object.

"Come, I'll show you. Might do you a bit of good to see how dangerous the real world is."

Despite your protests, Estelle drags you off the main street, turning off by the butcher's shop to travel down a long twisting alley.

The houses transform to gloomy apartments. Scraps of fabric cover broken windows, and a pair of stray roosters are crowing at one another by a grassless yard. A man has passed out in the middle of the sidewalk.

Willie taps you from within your pocket.

You see the mouse staring at the man and give the slumped figure a closer look. He's dressed in a respectable black jacket, but liquid seems to be shining on the back. His head slumps forward, green eyes wide and glassy. Someone has shoved a red apple into his mouth.

Estelle doesn't appear to have noticed anything amiss. There's a haughty smile on her face as she sees your expression, and she continues to walk toward the man. "Suppose seeing someone in this state would shock a wide-eyed youth like yourself. But a mature woman like myself is used to— Ahh!"

She breaks off in a sudden scream and stumbles backward, trying to get away from the man.

"He's dead!" she says.

Estelle grabs your arms. Her face is pale and anxious.

"Yes, he is," you reply, scarcely believing it yourself.

"I recognize him! That's Revered Bertrand Powers," she says. "There's blood all over the front of his shirt! I couldn't see it until I got closer. Someone must have stabbed him! The police here are useless. Promise me, you'll figure out what happened."

And here you thought Estelle didn't like your mystery solving skills.

Willie's head is already peeping out of your pocket. You suspect you were always going to get involved in this investigation.

Maybe finding the killer will make Estelle like you.

* * *

Estelle's screams attract the attention. There is a tall, gray building nearby. A group of half-dressed girls appear at the windows.

You hear scrambling within, and a police officer stumbles outside buttoning his pants. Soon, a crowd has gathered.

Willie slips out of your pocket to investigate while you comfort Estelle. Whispers start to rustle through the crowd.

"That's Reverend Bertrand Powers," someone says. "What's he doing outside Madam Appleseed's House? He's supposed to be a man of God."

"Those are the worst of the lot," a second voice whispers. "He must've done something worse than refuse to pay for Joy Appleseed to kill him."

"Why would you think it was her? I heard Reverend Powers was having an affair with Susan Small. She probably found out he was making trips down here and stabbed him herself."

"The butcher's wife and the reverend were having an

affair?" A new voice joins the conversation. "Harold Small's got a nasty temper. Someone ought to check on his wife. I wouldn't be surprised if he killed Reverend Powers and Susan!"

"Don't be ridiculous," the second voice objects. "That apple in his mouth is an obvious sign as to the killer."

"Careful, Joy might hear you accusing her," the first voice warns. "Anyway, I'll bet the real culprit is Reverend Hopewell. He's lost half his parishioners since Powers arrived."

Suddenly the police officer coughs loudly and turns to the crowd. "Well, nothing to see here folks. Just a street brawl gone wrong. Back to work with you all." He flicks his hands.

Gradually, the crowd disperses.

You're about to object, but you feel Willie jump onto your hand and wriggle up your shirt sleeve to your shoulder.

He whispers in your ear: "The officers are lying. They know that this was no street brawl. Whoever killed Reverend Powers wanted him dead. There were multiple stabs to his chest, all from a single, very large knife. I've got four suspects."

You have a feeling you know who they are.

SUSPECT #1: The Madam

"The police think Joy Appleseed is the killer," Willie tells you as you walk toward the large building outside of which the body was found. "But neither want to arrest her. I suspect both are frequenters of her establishment."

Feeling out of place, you knock on the crumbling wooden door. Someone has painted a pair of black lips biting into a shiny red apple above the entrance.

You hear giggling and a flurry of footsteps within. A young girl, accentuating her age with a pair of pigtails, opens the door.

There's a confused look on her face at the sight of you, but as if following a script, she says, "Welcome to Madam Appleseed's House of Pleasure where all your dreams can come true. What are you seeking?"

"I need to speak with Joy Appleseed."

The girl tries to explain that the Madam doesn't take visitors, but your conversation is overheard, and soon a tall, middle-aged woman arrives at the door. Her jaw is too broad to consider pretty, and there's gray streaks in her hair. She's dressed in a black silk robe with red apples embroidered on the hem and a tall pair of black boots beneath. Something silver flashes within. You think it might be a weapon, but the woman positions the long robe so you can't see.

After dismissing the girl, she runs her eyes over you and holds out her hand. "Joy Appleseed," she introduces herself. "I sense that you're not here for the usual reasons."

"Are you familiar with Reverend Bertrand Powers?" you ask.

There's a glint of fury in her eyes at the sound of his name, but she blinks it away, plastering a sad smile over her face like someone practiced in masking their emotions. "Everyone in Brightville knows Reverend Powers. He's the head of the largest congregation in the city. I suppose I should say was the head, given that he's been killed. My girls tell me that he was in a street brawl just outside my establishment. Terrible shame."

"Does that surprise you?"

One of her eyebrows rises in a cool, smooth arch. "That Reverend Powers was stabbed or that it happened so close to me?"

"Both."

"Stabbings are common around here. There's a lot of men

with knives down our alley. They're always looking for something to steal or a poor girl to overpower and control. Trick is to have the better weapon." There's a flicker of a smile on her lips, and she shuffles her boot. "Reverend Powers has become quite common around here too though it is unusual to see him here at this time of day."

"He visited your establishment?"

"In a sense." Joy Appleseed snorts. "The Reverend was on a mission to convert all the lost sheep of Brightville as he called us. He'd taken it upon himself to stand outside my establishment and preach, hoping to change the hearts of sinners. I might have admired his tenacity if he'd started anywhere else in the area. There's a gambling den, an opium house, and more than a few speakeasies. But of course, the reverend was more concerned about the souls of the attractive young women in my employ."

From her tone, it's obvious she thinks the Reverend's motives were less than pious.

"The worst part," she continues, "is that his efforts were attracting more of his kind."

You feel Willie nudge you and realize that there's something significant about this statement.

Joy Appleseed is hinting that there are other preachers in the area.

"Would that include someone like Reverend Michael Hopewell?" you ask.

Joy's jaw tightens in annoyance. "Yes. He's been even bolder in his attempts to save my girls than Bertrand was. But then, he's also more desperate for parishioners. His church was on the brink of collapse before Bertrand's death. Now, there'll be plenty of lost little lambs flocking toward Michael. Perhaps you ought to speak with him."

SUSPECT #2: The Butcher's Wife

After asking around, you learn the location of Michael Hopewell's home. However, in order to get to it, you have to walk back down the long twisting alley. Just as you're about to turn back onto the main street, Willie pokes his nose out and taps your side.

"Look there," the mouse says.

He's pointing to a small white building. It's the butcher's shop. A large sign out front advertises fresh meats. There's a trio of fruit trees growing beside it. One is full of red apples. A woman is in the garden, humming to herself as she gathers them in a basket. There are wet patches of sweat under her armpits, obvious in her loose white blouse.

"I think that might be Susan Small," Willie whispers. "The butcher's wife who was having an affair with Reverend Powers."

To test this theory, you call out to the woman in the garden.

Susan Small looks up the moment she hears her name.

You make your way toward her.

She has an oval face with wide-set eyes and cupid-bow lips. Only a few gray strands mixed with her dark curls betray her age. There's a red rim around her eyes, and snot glistens beneath her nose.

It looks like she's been crying.

Susan wipes her face with the edge of her gray sleeve and paints on a smile. "Can I help you with something?"

Her voice is sweet. She doesn't seem the type to murder a jilted lover, but looks can be deceiving.

You introduce yourself and launch straight into your first

question. "What's your relationship with Reverend Bertrand Powers?"

"I was one of his parishioners," she explains, then corrects herself. "But I'm afraid I have to find a new church now."

"Any particular reason?" you ask, wondering if she's aware that the Reverend is now dead.

"It was my husband's idea. He felt like Reverend Powers' sermons weren't connecting with him anymore. And I can't fault Harold. The Reverend has been focused on genesis a bit much recently. Anyways, it wouldn't be right to attend a different church to my husband." She gives you a broad, sweet smile.

"Are you sure your husband's request didn't have something to do with you and Reverend Powers' affair?"

Susan's eyes grow wide, and she drops the basket of apples in her hands. "How dare you accuse me of such a thing! I would never betray my marriage oaths in such a way. There are some nasty rumors going about this city. I try to turn the other cheek, but I know what they like to say about the Reverend and me. All because I volunteered to help him with managing his donations. There's nothing going on between us. He's just a friendly man with a tendency to be a bit... touchy at times."

Her lips close into a tight line. She looks uncomfortable, as though recalling an unpleasant memory, but she shakes her head, and the smile returns to her face. It looks forced.

"Reverend Powers treats all his parishioners exactly the same," she assures you, bending down to scoop up her apples. "I'm certainly nothing special. Now is that all or did you want to purchase some meat? My husband's just got a fresh set of pork. I'm sure he's finished preparing it by now."

For some reason, it looks like she might cry again.

SUSPECT #3: The Butcher

Stripped carcasses hang from windows and bright red flanks of meat sit on blocks of ice within the butcher's shop. There's no sign of Harold Small.

Willie reaches out of your pocket and presses a small silver bell on the counter.

"Just a minute," a loud voice comes from behind a black curtain.

A moment later a large man steps out. He's got a smooth face with a mop of red hair. There's a brown apron tied around him. It's covered in blood splatters, some drier than others. His dark gloves appear equally stained.

"What can I get for you?"

You explain that you're not there to purchase meat but to inquire about Reverend Bertrand Powers.

Harold's eyes narrow. "Why're you asking me about him?"

You get the sense that the wrong answer will get you thrown out of the shop. Thinking fast, you invent a story. "I'm new in Brightville and looking for a new parishioner. Your wife seems to quite like him, but you don't seem as keen."

Harold snorts and wipes his hands on his apron, trying and failing to get them clean. "Susan likes everyone. Kindest person I know. Can't even like to watch when I cut up the animals, faints on account of blood. I reckon she'd be a vegetarian if I'd let her. If you ask Susan about anyone in this city, she'll find the good."

"But what do you think of Reverend Powers?" you press.

Harold considers the question for a moment. Then he pulls a large carving knife from his apron. The flash of steel frightens you, and you stumble backward for a moment before your brain kicks in.

"He was a mountain lion. And poor Susan is a deer," Harold says, pointing the blade of his knife toward a carcass hanging behind him. He wipes the steel with the edge of his apron and looks back at you. "Now, are you going to buy something or not? There's no quail, but we've got a special on pork."

SUSPECT #4: The Other Reverend

After leaving the butcher's shop, you and Willie make your way a few streets over to a blue-painted lodging house. The landlady points you to the room on the second floor that Reverend Michael Hopewell is renting.

"If he even still counts as a Reverend," she says with a scoff. "Lost most of his parishioners to Reverend Powers. You ought to speak with him instead! Twice as handsome as Michael." She gives a dreamy sigh before, slaps her fist against the door, and disappears down the stairs.

You can hear someone stomping in the room, and a man's voice shouts, "Yes, I've got your money now, you thieving wench, but you're a day—"

Michael Hopewell stops as he opens the door and sees you there.

He's tall with a long, thin face, too gaunt to be considered attractive. His hairline is receding, and despite his bony limbs, he has a sizable stomach. He's wearing a pair of cotton trousers and slightly damp shirt that makes it look as though he's recently showered. But you notice flecks of blood on his boots.

"You're not my landlady," Reverend Hopewell says, stating the obvious. "What are you doing outside my door?"

You tell him a similar story to the one you told Harold Small, claiming to be new in town and in search of a congregation.

Reverend Hopewell's expression changes at once. He ushers you into his room.

It's a cramped space, thought not as bad as the crews' quarters on the steamboat. Stuffed deer heads adorn the walls. There's a large collection of knives displayed above a small mantle. A small bed is folded against a wall to make space for a little table and pair of chairs. In the center of the table, a meager fruit bowl displays a half-brown banana, a handful of shriveling grapes, and a pair of spotted green apples.

He sees you looking and offers you some. "Been meaning to go to the grocery store," he says. "But I went hunting today instead. Shot a few quail that I managed to sell." He points down to the splatters on his boots.

You and Reverend Hopewell sit opposite one another as he launches into a religious spiel. He takes one of the green apples and bites into it.

"Nice and tart," he says. "They're a bit bruised, but still good. Are you sure you don't want one?"

You shake your head, but seeing an opening, you ask him about the biblical significance of the apple.

"Giving into temptation, of course. It's the tale of Eve in the Garden of Eden. Don't you know Genesis?"

Before he can recite the entirety of it, you cut him off. "Can you tell me anything about Reverend Bertrand Powers? Someone else recommended him to me."

Reverend Hopewell digs his nails into his apple. "Powers is a performer, if you like that sort of thing. He's not really inter-ested in preaching so much as getting attention— especially from his female parishioners." He taps his nose as though letting you in on a secret. "I'll give you an example. Powers has been visiting some of the less savory areas of town, pretending to be on a mission to convert a group of wayward girls. But do you think he's really trying?"

Sensing the correct answer, you shake your head.

"No! Exactly!" Reverend Hopewell slams his hand down on the table, excited to have you on his side. "Now I went to the same establishment, not for the attention mind you, but because there was a seed of a good idea in Powers' selfishness. I tried to really rescue one of those girls from her predicament. Do you know what happened to me?"

Reverend Hopwell continues before you can answer.

"Joy Appleseed threatened to kill me if I ever returned! Pulled a gun out her shoe and waved it right in my face!"

He leans back as though exhausted just from the memory.

"Believe me," he says, managing to continue after a few deep breaths. "If Powers ever really tried to make a difference in those girls' lives, Appleseed would see to it that he was killed."

After you leave the apartment, Willie pokes his head from your pocket.

"Another job well done," he announces. "We'll just need to visit the police before heading back to the ship."

Your Answer

WHO KILLED REVEREND BERTRAND POWERS?

1. Joy Appleseed, the madam
2. Susan Small, the butcher's wife
3. Harold Small, the butcher
4. Michael Hopewell, the other reverend

If you need a hint, turn to the back of this book.
If you know the culprit, turn the page for the solution.

The Solution

Answer: Harold Small

WHEN YOU CONVINCE the two policemen at the station to listen, you inform them, "Reverend Bertrand Powers was murdered by the butcher, Harold Small."

The policemen exchange a look. It's clear that they're skeptical.

You explain, "Reverend Bertrand Powers was getting a little too friendly with some of his female practitioners. He made a pass at Susan Small. When Harold found out, he was furious. He told his wife that they were going to switch churches, but when he saw Reverend Powers pass by his street, Harold must have seen red. He followed the Reverend down the alley and confronted him in front of Madam Appleseed's establishment. If you check the stab wounds on Reverend Powers, you should find that they match perfectly with Harold's butcher knife."

This is enough information for the police to go and investigate. However, when you return to the ship and tell the story to your crewmates, Estelle has a lot of more questions.

"But what about the other three that you investigated? How'd you know it wasn't them?"

"Joy Appleseed threatened Reverend Hopewell with a gun," you answer. "If she was going to murder anyone, it's unlikely she'd use a knife.

"Susan Small hates the sight of blood, and she was crying just knowing that her husband was cutting up a pig. Even if she'd seen Reverend Powers go down the alley, it seems unlikely that she'd have easy access to her husband's knife or the ability to sneak up and stab him.

"Although Susan Small could have seen Reverend Powers go down the alley, much like her husband, it's not certain that she would've had access to the knives.

"Susan Small had access to her husband's knife, and could also have seen Reverend Powers go down the alley, but she faints at the sight of blood. She'd have been easy to catch if she'd stabbed the Reverend.

"Michael Hopewell, the other Reverend, had a strong motive, but there was nothing to indicate that he was lying about going hunting that morning. He said he'd shot and sold quail, and he had money to give his landlady. There was also no way for him to have known that Reverend Powers would be outside Madame Appleseed's at the time since he can't see the alley from his window. Plus, Hopewell prefers green apples to red.

"Beyond all of that, however, there was a single piece of evidence that clearly incriminated Harold Small.

"He accidentally spoke about Reverend Powers in past tense even though he shouldn't have known that the reverend was dead."

Estelle seems pleased by your work. You hope she might apologize for her previous cruelty.

"Not bad," the cleaner says. "Suppose everyone's got to be good at something."

She gives you a quick tap on the shoulder before wandering into the ship.

Case #6: The Bludgeoned Gossip

THE WHISTLE ANNOUNCES that you've docked at your next stop. It's the port of Smisper, a quaint little town with small painted homes and manicured lawns.

No one is more excited to be in Smisper than Gertie. Instead of helping the passengers like she's supposed to, she races off the SS Wilkinshire.

"She'll need talking to about that," Captain Ewan says with a sigh. This is obviously his domain, but he turns to you with a smile. "You can do it as First Mate."

You sigh but there's no sense arguing. The Captain seems to enjoy passing over the disciplining to you.

Once the passengers have left the SS Wilkinshire, you walk down the gangplank. Your usual friend is tucked into your pocket.

"Why is Gertie so excited to be in Smisper?" you ask, tucking your chin so that none of the people on the dock will think you're talking to yourself.

Willie's head peeps up at you. "Probably because of Eveleyn Leeky's gossip column," he explains. "She's the town's notorious gossip writer. She publishes a report every Friday.

Gertie enjoys reading all the drama that's happening in Smisper. She's probably gone running straight to one of the newsstands."

As usual, Willie is correct. You find Gertie at the first newsstand, right by the edge of the harbor. She's holding a pink piece of paper, eyes wide with excitement as she reads it.

You approach and clear your throat, trying to think how best to chastise her for her behavior.

Gertie looks up at you. There's a big grin on her face. "We've come to Smisper at the best possible time," she informs you, waving the pink piece of paper. "Evelyn Leeky is about to leak something big tomorrow. She's hinting at it in her last column. Read this!"

She shoves the pink piece of paper into your hands, pointing at the last paragraph.

I've recently learned a life-altering secret about a certain bespectacled redhead in our midst. She won't want it shared. But no one ever does. Trust me, readers, you won't want to miss next week's news.

"I can't wait to find out what it is!" Gertie squeals.

"Well, you'll be waiting a long time," the boy behind the newsstand informs her, looking up suddenly from his own magazine. "Evelyn Leeky's dead. Heard it a few minutes ago. Neighbor found her body and called the police just this afternoon."

"Dead?" Gertie's mouth is agape. "What happened?"

The boy leans closer, evidently pleased to have her attention on him instead of the papers, and lowers his voice. "Apparently, someone murdered her this morning."

Gertie turns to you.

You already know what she's going to say.

* * *

The police won't let you in when you get to the scene of the crime: Evelyn Leeky's house. But you have a secret investigator with you. Willie gives you a wink as he sneaks out of your pocket and through a gap in the window.

Gertie tries to argue with the police, telling them that you're a private investigator. They have little interest.

"Don't know where you're hearing that this is a murder, love," a baby-faced officer says, leaning against the door and giving Gertie a big smile. "But Ms. Leeky died from an allergic reaction. We found traces of orange in her lemonade. Nothing sinister about that."

Except that lemonade doesn't typically contain oranges.

While the police aren't interested in your assistance, someone else overhears and approaches you. It's a plain-faced middle-aged brunette wearing sensible shoes. She introduces herself as Wendy Jones.

"I'm Ms. Leeky's neighbor," she explains, pointing to her house. "I found her this afternoon. I had no idea she was allergic to oranges, but I did see the glass of lemonade on the desk beside her. Evelyn wasn't liked by too many people in the town. There's no doubt in my mind that someone killed her."

"Any idea as to who?" you ask.

"Not exactly, but I believe I can narrow it down for you. It's Thursday. Three people visit Evelyn every Thursday. Belinda Grouse, the beautician, drops off a set of cosmetic supplies. Hyacinth West, Evelyn's benefactor, collects the column that will be published the next day. And Lydia Moore, Evelyn's niece, stops by for tea, though that usually ends in arguing."

Assuming she's done, you thank her and go to leave, but Wendy grabs your arm.

"There's one more person who visited Evelyn today, however, Daisy Thorn. She's a housewife, no relationship with Evelyn that I know about. Evelyn's toy poodle, Fifi, started barking. It was the only time I've heard the poor little thing today. I happened to be by my window, so I looked outside and spotted Daisy entering the house."

"Ooh! This is getting juicy," Gertie says. She looks a little too excited given that there's been a murder.

"I haven't told you the most interesting thing about all of this yet."

* * *

As you get directions to each of your suspects' locations, you see Willie waving to you by the window of the house.

You excuse yourself and go to the mouse.

"What did you find out?"

He climbs up your hand onto your shoulder so that he can better whisper in your ear. "There were a few things I noticed that might be clues," he says.

You listen to Willie as he lists five observations:

1. There were feathers in the foyer entrance, the sitting room, and Evelyn's study.
2. Evelyn had a box in her sitting room with a large collection of cosmetics that she hadn't yet unpacked. None contained orange extract.
3. The lemonade on Evelyn's desk definitely contained orange extract. Willie could smell it. However, there was another half-finished glass of lemonade in the kitchen sink that did not contain orange extract.
4. There was lipstick on both glasses of unfinished lemonade. However, the lipsticks were different colors.
5. It appeared that someone had searched through Evelyn's study prior to the police's arrival.

"What have you learned?" Willie asks.

"I have the suspect list. Four women this time. And according to Evelyn's neighbor, all are redheads."

SUSPECT #1: The Beautician

There's a woman getting her hair styled in the beauty parlor as you arrive. You watch the beautician, a short woman with a strawberry-colored bun, finish arranging the customer's curls. You assume the beautician is Belinda Grouse, your first suspect.

The customer inquires about makeup. Belinda takes out a variety of tubes. She tests a couple of lipsticks on herself, showing the customer how she'll look. The third one she applies is a deep pink called Steal-my-heart.

Hidden behind your collar, Willie whispers into your ear, "That's the same lipstick that was on the glass in Evelyn's study."

Once the customer selects her color, Belinda applies it. She then sells the customer a tube of lipstick and two bottles of different lotions.

Finally, she turns to you. "Looking for something special?" She begins showing you products behind her counter. "I've just made a new batch of lemon-and-ginger body butter, orange-and-lime face scrub, and I have a new shipment of mascara."

"No thank you," you reply. "I'm here to talk about Evelyn Leeky."

Belinda presses her hand to her chest. "Yes, I heard. Such a tragedy! I was always so cautious to ensure that not a hint of orange slipped in when I made Evelyn's products. I can't believe her allergy got her in the end!"

"Did Evelyn purchase a lot of her products from you?"

"All of them as far as I know," Belinda says, turning from you and beginning to tidy up. "I delivered a small box to her every Thursday, first thing in the morning. She had dry skin and went through the lotions fast. A lot of my customers have that problem."

As she's tidying up, she lifts the tray of lipsticks up where you can see the full display.

Willie taps your neck. "Do you see the one called Pucker-up-pink?"

Your eyes scan the tubes and land on a pale peachy color. You nod.

"That's the lipstick that was on the glass in the sink."

Before Belinda can pack the tubes back, you grab the pucker-up-pink. "Is this a popular color?"

She purses her lips for a moment as she tries to think. "All my products are popular. I'm the only beautician in town. But I do have some customers who exclusively wear that one for a signature look. I prefer to try different options myself. I like that for daytime, but something darker is better at night. Want me to show you?"

You get the sense that she's hoping to make a sale.

With a sigh, you reach into your pocket, take out a bit of change, and offer it to Belinda in exchange for the lipstick.

It's cheaper than you would've thought, which is a pleasant surprise.

"Can you tell me what happened this morning when you met with Evelyn?" you ask, slipping the tube into your pocket.

"It was the same as always. I passed the box to her at the door, patted Fifi's head, and told her I was excited to see her column tomorrow. Then I got back in my car and drove off. I don't normally linger when I'm making deliveries."

Another customer comes in looking to purchase some lotions, and Belinda's attention shifts.

You slip out the door, planning to visit the next redhead on your list.

SUSPECT #2: The Benefactor

Hyacinth West's house is easy to find. It's a massive white manor with Grecian columns, quite out of place among the quaint, colorful houses of Smisper.

You walk up and raise your hand.

Before you can knock, the door opens. A woman in her mid-sixties steps out. She's wearing a white feather jacket with a fascinator to match. There's a long string of pearls around her neck, and a pair of dark stilettos on her feet.

Her hair is a bright vibrant red.

There's no doubt in your mind. This is Hyacinth West, Evelyn's wealthy benefactor.

Hyacinth has been twice widowed, and rumors about her husbands' deaths surface every few weeks. You've asked around, however, and Evelyn Leeky never wrote about her benefactor in her gossip column.

"Whatever you're selling, I'm not interested in buying," Hyacinth says, sweeping past you. "I have to get to the printer."

You follow her down the long driveway, trying to guess why Evelyn's former benefactor would be on her way to the printer. "Do you have Evelyn's last column?"

"I wish! People in this town might buy two copies in that case," Hyacinth says. "But I'm sure news of her death will be just as juicy. I had one of my assistants whip something up that will hopefully tantalize the town."

"Did you visit Evelyn's house yesterday?"

Feathers fly from Hyacinth's jacket as she walks. She stops before a black vehicle, parked at the edge of her property. You're worried that you might lose her.

"Are you a reporter?" she asks, eyebrows rising.

"I'm the First Mate on the SS Wilkinshire."

Hyacinth laughs. "That's a new one. Get in."

To your surprise, she opens the door to her car. It's a new Model A.

You're barely in the passenger seat when she starts the engine, and soon you're zipping along the narrow Smisper roads. Her foot is heavy on the gas, and her eyes are reluctant to see pedestrians.

You hold your breath, hoping that the printer is close.

"So, you're curious about Evelyn," Hyacinth says, whipping around a blind corner. "A lot of people are. That's the danger of celebrity. Even though Evelyn was writing about others, there were always people wanting to know more about the woman behind the pen, some with more nefarious intentions than others. That's why she kept her orange allergy so secret. Of course, I thought she was being overdramatic, but I suppose she was right in the end."

You flinch as the car flies toward a pedestrian. Luckily, the walker jumps out of the street before another tragedy occurs.

Lump rising in your throat, you manage to ask, "What happened the last time you saw Evelyn?"

"Nothing of much interest. It was this morning. I went to collect the column like always, but she said she wasn't finished, which was unusual. Evelyn always gets her work in on time. I wasn't impressed with the delay. I asked to see what she was doing, but she said she hadn't started yet. I insisted she begin right away, and she tried to argue that she needed to unpack a box of cosmetics that had just been delivered! Can you imagine? Of course, we argued. I told her if I came back this afternoon and found unpacked cosmetics but no column, I was going to withdraw her funding."

The car jerks to a sudden halt, and you almost fly into the windshield.

Hyacinth continues without concern, "Evelyn was obviously procrastinating. I think she may have been suffering some sort of moral crisis. Or she didn't want me to see the column."

She climbs out her car, leaving enough feathers on the seat to build a swan.

You stay in the passenger seat for a moment, hand to your chest, trying to stop your heart from racing.

SUSPECT #3: The Niece

Lylah Moore lives further outside of the town. You assume that you'll need to take a car to get there and decide to let Gertie know before leaving Smisper.

Your gossip-loving crew member wanted to stay with Wendy Jones while you investigated. Gertie claimed walking all around town would tire her feet. You suspect she wanted to keep an eye on what the police were doing and hear any additional information that Evelyn's neighbor might have.

As you turn down the street, you can hear a small, high-pitched bark. It doesn't seem to be stopping.

When you arrive at Evelyn's house, you see the source of the noise. Evelyn's toy poodle, Fifi, is barking at a young, red-haired woman who's speaking with the police.

"See?" The woman says. "I told you. Fifi doesn't like me.

And I've no interest in the box of lotions either. They're terrible quality. Give them to someone else, and have them take the dog as well. She'll need a good home."

One of the policemen scratches his head. "But you're Evelyn's closest relative."

Guess you won't need to leave the town after all.

The red-headed woman is none other than Lylah Moore, Evelyn's niece. She's dressed in men's trousers and a plain blouse. Her red hair has been pulled back in a short tail behind her head, and there's no hint of make-up on her face. From a distance, someone might mistake her for a man.

The toy poodle continues barking while Lylah argues with the policemen.

Finally, Gertie runs up and offers to take the puppy.

Somehow, you don't see Captain Ewan agreeing to a dog on the SS Wilkinshire. He'll probably make you be the bad guy.

But you decide to give Gertie her few minutes of delight with the poodle, who's somehow warmed up to a complete stranger faster than her previous owner's niece.

Lylah is starting to leave. You need to catch her before she does.

"Excuse me," you say, hurrying toward her as she walks down the street. "I was wondering if I could ask you some questions about your aunt."

"No." Her voice is gruff.

"Please, they'll be short. I'm just trying to figure out what happened to her."

"I can tell you the answer to that," Lylah says, not turning to look at you. "My aunt was a spineless gossip who wrote a column that angered the whole town. Someone who's secret she revealed learned about her orange allergy and decided to kill her off."

Judging from Fifi's response to Lylah and her own description of her aunt, it doesn't sound like she was close to Evelyn. The information surprises you.

"You visited your aunt every Thursday. Why would you do that if you disliked her so much?"

"Sympathy," Lylah says. Suddenly she stops at the street corner.

You almost run into her.

"No, I'm lying," Lylah admits, finally turning to face you. "That's what I told myself to feel better about it. The truth is that I visited my aunt because I hoped that a sense of closeness would ensure she never revealed any of my secrets. So much for that."

Is Lylah admitting what you think?

"Are you saying that it's your secret Evelyn was going to reveal tomorrow?"

She nods.

"That gives you an obvious motive for murder," you point out.

"Definitely," Lylah agrees. "Except that I'm not a killer. After realizing that she was going to reveal my secret, I vowed never to speak with her again. I haven't seen her since last Thursday when I saw her column."

"So where were you today?"

"At my house outside of town," Lylah says. "I have a small farm that I share with my roommate, Moira. She can confirm that I was there."

SUSPECT #4: The Housewife

Daisy Thorn lives in a bright blue house surrounded by buildings that would be identical were it not for the variety of colors. Each has white cookie-cutter trim around its roof and a small patio.

However, only Daisy's house has a garbage bin out in front of it.

Willie notices it too.

"Before you knock on the door, let me have a look in the trash," he suggests.

You carry him to the bin and lift the lid.

The mouse roots around for a moment. You wait, glad he's the one doing this task and not you.

"I found something!" Willie says, emerging from the trash with a pink piece of paper clutched in his paws.

You lift both him and it out of the bin. Your eyes scan the paper.

Handwritten on the back of one of Evelyn's old columns is a rough draft of her never finished product. Lylah was correct. It is about her. Evelyn was planning to reveal that Lylah was in a romantic relationship with her female roommate.

Or perhaps she wasn't. The draft is full of slashes, cutting away most of the crucial information and notes on the side suggest that Evelyn was brainstorming other ideas.

Had Evelyn survived, she might have changed her mind about revealing her niece's secret.

"Come on," Willie says, pulling you out of your thoughts. "We need to talk to Daisy. I have a lot of questions about how she got this."

Willie's right.

You fold the column, slip it into your pocket, and knock on Daisy's door.

A young woman with a baby strapped to her chest opens the door. She's wearing a long, blue house dress. Her pale red hair is braided and pinned in a crown around her head. Her lips are painted a pale pink that you can now identify as pucker-up-pink.

Before you can introduce yourself, Daisy smiles and pulls you inside. She seems delighted by the prospect of even an unfamiliar visitor.

Daisy seats you at a small, circular table in her kitchen, right between two high chairs. There's another young child playing in the sitting area. You can hear him making plane noises for his toy.

You finally manage to introduce yourself while Daisy offers you an assortment of baked goods to try. It's only when you mention Evelyn Leeky that your hostess' demeanor changes. Her grip tightens around the spatula in her hand until her knuckles turn white.

"I was very sorry to hear about Evelyn's death. But I'm afraid I didn't know her well. My father and my husband will be looking into it."

"Your father and your husband?" This is news to you.

"My father is the chief of police, and my husband is on the force," she says, giving you a robotic smile. "Sure you won't take a slice of pumpkin pie?" She holds the dish before you.

Judging from the look in her eyes, you're worried what might happen if you turn it down.

"Evelyn was a lovely lady, and we're all very sorry to lose her here in Smisper," she says, slicing the pie with an unnecessarily large knife, apparently unconcerned that her baby might grab it.

"Do you know how she died?" You ask, easing your hand into your pocket. You want to confront her with the evidence you found earlier, but it might be best to wait until she's put the knife down.

"Allergic reaction, I've heard," Daisy says. "Probably some sort of peanut snuck into a package of something she was eating. I've a cousin who's deathly allergic to nuts, and he has to be so careful."

"When did you last see Evelyn?"

"I don't know. Maybe a few weeks ago?" Daisy finally puts her knife in the sink and presents you with a slice of pie.

"Then how did you end up with this?" you ask, pulling the evidence from your pocket and jumping up, just in case you need to flee a knife-swinging housewife with a baby slung around her chest.

Daisy's eyes go wide as she sees the pink piece of paper. Her mouth opens and closes like a goldfish. Then, her face contorts in an almost exaggerated expression of despair. She drops to one of the chairs, earning a soft, disgruntled moan from the baby.

The only one on the verge of sobbing, however, is Daisy.

"I can explain," she tells you. "I swear, I didn't kill Evelyn. She was already dead when I went there."

You cross your arms, waiting for the rest of Daisy's story.

"You can't tell anyone, but about a month ago, I bought a bottle of whiskey. It was terrible, I know, given my father and my husband's positions, but I've been so depressed taking care of the kids all alone. I just needed to blow off some steam.

When I saw Evelyn's column next week, I was certain she was referring to me. I thought she was going to reveal my secret! It would be just terrible for my family if that happened. So, I asked my mother to watch the kids and slipped out to see Evelyn just before noon. I was hoping I could convince her to write about someone else.

The door was open, so I let myself in. Her poodle barked once or twice, but she settled down quickly, and I called out for Evelyn. When she didn't answer, I decided to look around myself. And that's when I found her, lying dead in her study.

I know I should've called the police but, I mean, how would I explain what I was doing in her house? So instead, I looked around for her column, found it, and ran. It's only when I got home that I realized the secret hadn't been about me at all."

"Was there a box of cosmetics when you arrived?"

"Oh yes," Daisy confirms. "I considered taking it. I go through mine so fast, but I'm not a thief. Swear." She crosses her heart.

"What about any feathers?"

Daisy tries to think for a moment. "There may have been some in the sitting room now you mention it. I didn't pay much attention. What have feathers got to do with Evelyn's death?"

"Possibly nothing," you say, moving your pumpkin pie onto a napkin and carrying it out the door.

* * *

Outside the house, Willie taps his tiny foot on your shoulder.

"Give me a taste of your pie," the mouse says. His eyes are wide as he looks at it.

"Can it wait?" you say.

He sighs. "I suppose. Let's head back to Evelyn's house. Hopefully the police will still be there, and we can tell both them and Gertie what happened."

Your Answer

WHO KILLED EVELYN LEEKY?

1. Belinda Grouse, the beautician
2. Hyacinth West, the benefactor
3. Lylah Moore, the niece
4. Daisy Thorn, the housewife

If you need a hint, turn to the back of this book.
If you know the culprit, turn the page for the solution.

The Solution

Answer: Belinda Grouse

WHEN YOU RETURN to Evelyn's house, the police are still there. So, to your surprise, is Lylah Moore, who's returned to give Gertie a list of things she'll need to do to properly care for Fifi.

You interrupt all of them with a loud cough. "Excuse me, but while you've been figuring out how to distribute the deceased's belongings, I've figured out who killed her." You pause for dramatic effect, waiting for all of them to be watching you before announcing. "Evelyn Leeky was killed by Belinda Grouse."

"The beautician who makes and sells cosmetics?" The nearest policeman's eyebrows rise. "Why would she want to murder Evelyn Leeky?"

Having discussed this with Willie on your walk over, you're quite certain you now know the answer.

"Because Belinda Grouse has been watering down all of her scrubs and lotions. That's how she's able to sell her products so cheap. She knows her customers will need to use more and will end up buying more as a result. She thought Evelyn learned her secret and was planning to expose her.

"This morning, when she visited Evelyn, instead of passing the cosmetics to her at the door, Belinda came inside. She must've said she was thirsty, so Evelyn took her into the kitchen for a glass of lemonade. When Evelyn wasn't looking, Belinda managed to sneak some orange extract into what remained in the pitcher. That's why, if you check the glass in the sink, I believe you'll find the orange-free lemonade with one of Belinda's lipsticks around the rim."

"And how did you figure out it wasn't one of the others?" Gertie asks, turning toward you. She has the same expression as earlier when she was reading the gossip column.

"As Evelyn's benefactor, Hyacinth has the weakest motive. Even if Evelyn had found dirt on her, Hyacinth could've used her money to ensure the story never saw the light of day. But on top of that, Hyacinth never had the opportunity to add anything to the lemonade. She didn't go into Evelyn's kitchen, or there would have been feathers everywhere.

Lylah is obviously innocent. She never visited her aunt today. Otherwise, Evelyn's neighbor would've heard Fifi bark more than once.

Daisy can't be the killer because she never knew about Evelyn's orange allergy."

One of the police officer's eyebrows rise so high that they're hidden by his cap. "My wife was a suspect?"

"Never mind that," you assure him. "She's been cleared. But you might want to spend a bit more time helping her with your children."

"You are absolutely brilliant!" Gertie declares, running up and tossing her arms around you in a hug.

She almost knocks Willie off of your shoulder, but he ducks against your back.

"I'm glad you think so, Gertie," you say. "But I'm afraid

you can't keep Fifi on the ship. Captain Ewan won't allow it, and Fifi really ought to go with Lylah."

"Oh no," Lylah objects. "I've already said that I can't take her. My aunt hated me, and she trained her dog to do the same."

"It will take some time for you and Fifi to grow accustomed to one another," you admit. "But your aunt didn't hate you. I don't believe she ever intended to publish your secret."

You show her Evelyn's handwritten notes that Willie found in Daisy's bin.

Lylah takes them in. Water fills in her eyes. "Maybe she would've done the right thing," she concedes. Then, with a sigh, she holds her arms out to Gertie. "I'll take Fifi. Moira will love her at least."

Fifi barks in objection for a few moments as she's passed to Lylah, but eventually she settles down. As they walk off, you see the poodle lick the face of her new owner.

They're going to be just fine together.

But you have a different problem now, you realize as Gertie loops her arms through yours and begins guiding you through the town. You still need to chastise her about running off the ship.

Case #7: The Blackmailers

IT'S your last night docked in Smisper, and the crew is supposed to do a thorough cleaning and inspection of the SS Wilkinshire before a group of guests board tomorrow morning. However, as you walk around the ship taking inventory, you spot your crew relaxing. Estelle is soaking her feet in a tub in the dining room. Gertie is in her cabin, giggling over letters from her sister. Biggie and Joe are on the deck throwing dice.

You look at Willie, who's riding in your pocket and helping you take inventory with his excellent memory. "Does it seem like the crew are doing even less than usual?"

"They've never been the most dedicated workers," Willie admits. "But they've been getting even worse the past few weeks. I wonder if something's going on."

You can't take care of the entire steamship on your own. You decide to take the issue up with Captain Ewan.

He's at least working, cleaning the steering wheel at the front of the boat. There's an open flask beside him. You suspect what's within is something stronger than soda.

At the sound of your footsteps, Captain Ewan sits up, bumping the top of his head against the wheel. "Ah, there's my trusty First Mate! I've been meaning to come see you. Any chance you could check on the boilers for me."

This is exactly the problem.

"That's Biggie's job," you remind him. "He ought to be down there now. And Estelle should be cleaning your steering wheel. Joe should be washing the dishes in the kitchen. And Gertie should be... well, she ought to be doing something!"

"Absolutely right," Captain Ewan agrees, lifting his hat to rub his forehead. He looks at you with sheepish eyes. There's a pink tinge to his nose. "Any chance you can tell them that?"

It doesn't make sense. Why does the Captain keep passing off all disciplinary action to you?

"You're the Captain," you remind him. "You ought to give the orders. Why do you keep letting them get away with everything."

Captain Ewan sighs. He takes a sip from his flask. "I'm going to share a secret with you. But promise, you won't think less of me as a Captain."

He leans closer, and you can smell the thick scent of moonshine on his breath.

"Captain, I'm sure whatever it is, I won't think less of you."

* * *

Once you've reassured Captain Ewan, he takes you to his cabin. It's twice the size of yours, with a double bed, a closet, coffee table, and desk.

Whoever designed the SS Wilkinshire was not an egalitarian when it came to room size.

You take a seat on one of the two chairs that fit in his room. There's the slight hint of brackish water in the cushions.

Captain Ewan goes through the items on his desk and pulls out four pieces of paper. He tosses them onto the table.

"The crew are blackmailing me," he admits with a sigh. "I can't discipline them or they'll get my Captain's license revoked, or worse, send news to my wife."

Willie peeps out from his pocket, trying to read the letters with you. There's no question that each is from a different crew member. The handwriting in each instance is quite unique. But the messages are vague and none are signed.

"But Captain, what information are they blackmailing you with?"

"Oh each crew member has some dirt on me," the Captain admits, sinking onto his bed with a sigh. He takes another sip of moonshine. "And I have dirt on them too. I was planning to use it to counter their blackmail, but the problem is that my memory is so bad, I can't remember which crew member committed what crime. I can't even remember what information they have on me."

From within your pocket, you hear Willie mutter, "He must remember something. We'll use whatever information he can muster to help him."

"Did you say something?" Captain Ewan asks, looking up from his flask and giving you an odd look.

Willie ducks back into your pocket, and you give the Captain your most innocent smile. "I was just saying that I'm going to help you. Tell me everything that you can remember."

Captain Ewan scratches his beard, trying to think. "Well, there are a few things I recall.

"One of the crew members is lying to their family about their current job title.

"One of the crew members cheated at cards at a speakeasy. They witnessed me break a very valuable vase at the bar that same night. We left before anyone noticed either our deceptions.

"One of the crew members accidentally killed one of their sibling's pet roosters. They weren't on the ship when I threw up in Joe's pot. The messages in all caps are definitely being sent by someone who's aware of neither of those incidents.

"Neither of the women accidentally killed a rooster.

"The crew member with the tiny handwriting is either the one who cheated in the speakeasy card game or the one who stole a ham from a butcher and framed his apprentice. Whoever it is, they definitely saw me throw up in Joe's pot!

"Estelle doesn't know about the time that I stole... I mean, borrowed... a horse and forgot to pay.

"The crew member who killed the rooster also wasn't there when I accidentally hit another boat.

"Both Gertie and Biggie are blackmailing me about incidents that occurred on the ship.

"Biggie's letters must be the ones in blue! He always writes in blue ink.

"I wish I could remember which crew member has the cursive writing."

You've tried to write down as much information as possible, but your mind feels scrambled from the Captain's stream of seemingly random facts. You promise to do your best and leave to speak with the crew, but before you've gone far, Willie pokes his head out.

"Why didn't you tell the Captain which crew member committed each crime, what information they're blackmailing him with, and which handwriting is theirs? He gave you more than enough information to figure it out!"

"Really?" You scratch your head and take out your notes to solve this puzzle.

Your Answer

WHAT INFORMATION CAN you deduce about the blackmailers? Fill in the grid!

Crew Member	Handwriting	Blackmailing the <u>Captain</u> for...	Guilty of...
Biggie			
Estelle			
Gertie			
Joe			

The Solution

WILLIE IS RIGHT! There's no need to speak to each of the crew. Captain Ewan gave you enough information to solve his problem.

You rush back into his room and show him your notes:

Crew Member	Handwriting	Blackmailing the Captain for...	Guilty of...
Biggie	Blue	Hitting a ship (probably while drinking)	Lying about his job title to his family
Estelle	Caps	Breaking an expensive vase at a speakeasy	Cheating at cards and keeping the money she won
Gertie	Tiny	Throwing up in Joe's pot	Stole a ham from a butcher and framed his innocent apprentice
Joe	Cursive	Stealing a horse	Killing his sibling's pet rooster

"Wow!" Captain Ewan looks surprised to see you back already. "I thought I'd given you an impossible task. I guess I have no excuse for not confronting the crew about their poor behavior now."

There's something strange about the Captain's tone.

Is he really that forgetful or was he just looking for an excuse to have you discipline everyone?

Either way, you've solved the puzzle and forced his hand. The task of chastising the crew is off your shoulders.

At least for now.

Hints

CASE #1: THE CAPTAIN'S GIFT
Hint: Only one crew member was likely to go into the room and discover the gift.

CASE #2: A MYSTERIOUS DROWNING
Hint: Follow the swans.

CASE #3: THE SPEAKEASY SHOOTING
Hint: Focus on the watch.

CASE #4: THE CASE OF THE STOLEN SILVERWARE
Only one person told the truth both times, and only the thief lied twice. This means that everyone else told one truth and one lie.

Start by figuring out who told the truth both times.

. . .

Here, in brief, are the statements given by your crewmates:

JOE: I was in my cabin when the silverware vanished. It was Captain Ewan who took it.

CAPTAIN EWAN: Joe is one who took the silverware. It definitely wasn't Gertie, because I'd sent her into town.

ESTELLE: It wasn't me. I spent the morning alone cleaning the cabins, and I was the only one there.

BIGGIE: I was busy all morning cleaning the boilers. It wasn't Captain Ewan, because he was up on the quarterdeck patrolling this morning.

GERTIE: Biggie is lying about working on the boilers. It wasn't me: the Captain sent me into town to purchase fresh supplies.

CASE #5: A MURDER MOST HOLY

Hint: The killer made a big mistake when giving an opinion on Reverend Bertrand Powers.

CASE #6: THE BLUDGEONED GOSSIP

Hint: Given that all of our suspects are redheads, they all had a motive to kill Evelyn. It's just a question of who had the opportunity to add orange to her lemonade.

CASE #7: THE BLACKMAILERS

This is a classic logic puzzle. Using a grid to match the different items can be very helpful.

		Handwriting				The Captain's Crimes				The Crews' Crimes			
		Blue	Cursive	Tiny	All Capitals	Hitting another boat	Breaking a vase	Throwing up in Joe's pot	"Borrowing" a horse	Cheating at cards	Lying about their job	Stealing a ham	Killing a pet rooster
Crew Members	Biggie												
	Estelle												
	Gertie												
	Joe												
The Crews' Crimes	Cheating at cards												
	Lying about their job												
	Stealing a ham												
	Killing a pet rooster												
The Captain's Crimes	Hitting another boat												
	Breaking a vase												
	Throwing up in Joe's pot												
	"Borrowing" a horse												

Volume 2

If you enjoyed this book, you'll want to pick up Steamboat Willie Whistlestop Puzzle Mysteries, Volume 2.

Turn the page for a sneak peek!

STEAM B⬤AT WILLIE

Vol. 2

WHISTLESTOP
PUZZLE MYSTERIES

*Seven exciting puzzles
for you to solve!*

HANNAH DOVE

Case #1: The Toxic Treacle Tart

＊

WHEN THE PASSENGERS board in Smisper the next morning, there's a familiar face among them.

Dressed in a fine fur coat despite the heat is none other than Hyacinth West, the wealthy widow who was once Evelyn Leeky's benefactor. She spots you, smiles, and waves.

"Well if it isn't the curious First Mate of the SS Wilkinshire," she says by way of greeting. She puts an arm around your shoulder and kisses both your cheeks, catching you off guard with her familiarity. "I was hoping I might run into you again on my voyage. I'm having a special dinner tonight with my little group. We're celebrating my engagement." She flashes you a large diamond.

Your eyebrows rise. This must be a recent development. You're certain that there was no ring on Hyacinth's finger when you spoke with her two days ago.

"You must come to my dinner tonight," Hyacinth tells you. "Not as a crew member, but as my guest. I've rented one of the SS Wilkinshire's private rooms."

Before you can decline, Hyacinth dashes away.

You intend to find her later and explain that you won't be

able to attend. But Willie's nose peeks from your pocket the moment the wealthy widow has left.

"We must go," he says, whiskers twitching. "There might be cheese."

* * *

You feel out of place in the SS Wilkinshire's private dining room. Even the nicest outfit you brought from home seems shabby compared to the other diners at the table. It doesn't help that you're attempting to tear off bits of cheese and sneak them under the table without anyone noticing.

There are five individuals at the table with you.

Hyacinth sits at the head. Beside her is her new finance, David Southland. He can't be much more than thirty. He sips a glass of juice which stains the tips of his pale mustache with a light pink.

Next to David is Christina Maxwell, Hyacinth's secretary. She's a very thin blonde with pinched lips and a pointed nose. Her hands flutter when she talks. More than once you notice them land on David's hand before pulling away.

At the end of the table is Hyacinth's cousin, Madeline Thorpe. The two women appear to be close in age. However, where Hyacinth's hair remains mostly red, Madeline's waves have conceded to the gray, with only a hint of the original black remaining. She wears a modest, unadorned blue dress, but her fingers fidget with a string of white pearls in her pocket.

The final guest is Hyacinth's daughter, Nora West. She sits between you and her mother. Her auburn hair is clipped behind her head, and a pair of spectacles perch on the end of her nose. She looks older than her mother's fiance, but it's difficult to tell. There's a greenish complexion to Nora's skin and she keeps pressing her hand to her stomach.

"The chef's done an excellent job with the steak," Hyacinth announces, filling an awkward silence that's descended over the table.

"And the parsley on the rice is divine!" Madeline adds

"It's basil," Nora snaps, brushing an auburn wave from her face and adjusting her glasses. "With a hint of mint."

"Oops." Madeline gives an apologetic shrug. "I thought I saw the chef take out a jar of parsley."

"Can't you see the difference?" Nora snaps.

An anxious look crosses Madeline's face, and you can see her fingers twist tight around the pearls in her pocket.

You think she's about to apologize, but Hyacinth waves her hand in dismissal and takes the attention from her cousin. "Basil, mint, parsley. They're all the same. Don't you all agree?"

Across the table, you see Christina nudge David with her elbow.

He jumps in his seat. "Yes definitely. All the same," he agrees, head bobbling on his neck. "I saw parsley in the kitchen too. Maybe it's you who's mistaken, Nora. You can't have eaten more than a bite of the rice anyway."

This is true. Unlike the rest of the dinner party, Nora has barely touched her food.

She scowls. "I'm not judging by the taste. I can tell from the leaf. I'd think everyone here would know better than to debate me on herbs."

David glances at Christina as though she might respond on his behalf. The secretary, however, is staring straight down, tapping her empty plate with a fork.

Hyacinth rests a hand on her fiancé's arm. He looks startled by the contact.

"David Darling," she says. "Nora is a botanist. She's very bright and excellent at her job."

"Oh. I see," David mumbles.

Nora snorts. "You're marrying a man who doesn't even know what your daughter does for a living. Have you thought this through at all?"

A dark look comes over Hyacinth's face, and there's something sinister about her smile. "Trust me, I have thought everything about this dinner through. Once dessert arrives, I have a surprise in store."

The uncomfortable silence settles on the table once more.

To your surprise, Madeline Thorpe breaks it. In a timid voice, she says, "I do think you have a point, Nora. The wedding feels a bit… rushed."

David and Christina both look started by the comment. Hyacinth gives her cousin a cold look. "Really? Because I think I have a tendency to—"

Before she can finish, Joe walks in, pushing a dinner tray before him. "Dessert is served," he says.

The chef gives you an amused look. Then his gaze lands on David, and he smiles. "Ah, the lost fiance," he says. "Glad you found your way from the kitchen."

David gives a nervous laugh.

"Now, the dessert is chocolate cupcakes and mini pecan pies. But I've included a special treacle tart just as you requested, Ms. Maxwell," Joe addresses Christina as he lifts the silver cover from the tray to reveal three layers of sweets.

The tapered tray rises from cupcakes, to pies, until arriving at the tiny top layer, which holds a single treacle tart.

"Don't worry, Ms. Thorpe. There's no walnuts in the pies, so they're safe for you to eat," Joe informs Madeline. "Now, I do hope you all enjoy dessert!" With a flourish of his chef's cap, he exits the room.

"Dinner and a show," Nora mutters under her breath, apparently unimpressed by Joe's friendly demeanor. She reaches toward the platter but changes her mind, prodding at the unfinished rice on her plate instead.

"Why is there only one treacle tart?" David whispers to Christina.

Before she can answer, Hyacinth speaks. "Would you like it, David?"

His nose wrinkles, and he shakes his head. "I can't stand the taste of treacle."

Christina nudges him again, an anxious look on her face. "But you know that they're Hyacinth's favorite," she hisses at him. With a nervous laugh, she turns to her boss. "David is playing coy. He asked me to have them make this one as a special treat for you."

"Oh how lovely!" Madeline says, already nibbling on a pecan pie. "You do love treacle tarts!"

"As everyone knows," Nora says, cutting her eyes toward David.

"Yes, I do," Hyacinth admits, hand inching toward it. "But if I'm going to get married, I ought to diet for the wedding. Don't you think, Christina?"

The secretary shuffles under Hyacinth's gaze. "Yes, of course," she agrees with another nervous laugh. "How silly of me! I'll eat it so it doesn't tempt you."

Christina grabs the treacle tart and takes a bite. There's another awkward silence, and you're wondering if to grab the last of the cheese on your dinner plate and then take your leave. You've had more than enough stilted dinner conversation for the evening.

As you start to push your chair back, however, you notice Christina's pupils suddenly expand. She clutches her throat and keels over, face down on the half-eaten treacle tart.

Plotworks Publishing

BE sure to visit our store at www.plotworkspublishing.com to discover this and many other titles to enjoy!

www.ingramcontent.com/pod-product-compliance
Lightning Source LLC
Chambersburg PA
CBHW052012170626
46808CB00007B/2889